Lone Star Holiday

Jolene Navarro

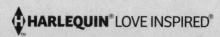

Recycling programs
for this product may
not exist in your area.

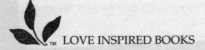

LOVE INSPIRED BOOKS

ISBN-13: 978-0-373-87846-8

LONE STAR HOLIDAY

www.Harlequin.com

Printed in U.S.A.

Come to me, all you who are weary and burdened,
and I will give you rest.
—*Matthew* 11:28

To Granner, JoAnn Hutchinson,
for sharing her faith and love of writing.
For Katrina, Storm, Tate and Bridger, thank you
for all the dinners cooked and dishes washed.
My greatest joy is being your mother.
To Fred for being you and allowing me to be me.

Chapter One

Lorrie Ann's sports car hugged the curves of the country road. Fence posts and cattle flew past her window as she ran back to the small town she fled twelve years ago. No one had warned her that in the pursuit of fame and fortune she could become emotionally and spiritually bankrupt. She glanced at the Bible with the purple tattered note sticking out of it. Well, her aunt might have, but she had been too stubborn to listen.

On the soft leather seat, next to the Bible, her cell vibrated again. Brent's face filled the screen. How did she ever find her now-ex-fiancé's grin charming? For two years she had ignored his behavior—until yesterday. Their last fight had escalated to the point where he'd hit her. When had she become her mother? Relationships were not her thing, and the situation with Brent proved her right.

That was the moment she took a long hard look at her life and didn't like what she saw. She had no one to turn to. They shared the same friends. He played the drums for the band she managed.

She hadn't taken a vacation in three years. With the holidays coming up she'd called the lead singer of the band she managed and told her she was heading home. Where was home? With nowhere to go, she headed to the only place she had family—her aunt's pecan farm in Clear Water, Texas. She couldn't imagine anyplace more different than Los Angeles.

The phone went quiet only to start chiming again a moment later. Teeth gritted, she shifted gears and picked up speed. She didn't want to hear his apologies.

A burst of anger had her grabbing the phone and throwing it out the window. She dashed past the green sign that said Clear Water was eight miles. She turned up the music and pushed down on the gas pedal only to have the engine sputter and jerk. The steering wheel became stiff under her hands. With all her muscle she forced the BMW to the side of the road.

She checked the gauges and sighed. No gas, no phone, and she only had herself to blame.

One moment of temper had caused her to chuck her phone out of her car. Now she could walk the eight miles to town or walk back to find her phone—and hope that it still worked.

She needed to make the call she had been avoiding anyway, so she started the hike to find her phone.

Lorrie Ann fought to keep her balance as she walked back up the hill she had just driven down. Her five-inch-heel boots, designed for flat city life, didn't take well to the rocky hike across the uneven ground.

The cool breeze whispered over her shoulders. She adjusted her brown felt fedora and glanced around the vast landscape of the Texas Hill Country. The Black Angus cows stopped chewing and silently watched her stumble along the fence. With one hand on the rough cedar post, she stared back. "What are you looking at?"

Great—less than a day back in Texas and she was talking to cattle. Closing her eyes, she took a deep breath. "Dear God, I know for the last twelve years I put You in the backseat, and now I'm asking for help every time I turn around. Please, just give me the peace to know You're in control and

I'm doing the right thing." Peace. She doubted she'd recognize it if it turned out to be a rattlesnake about to bite her.

A loud engine broke the endless silence of rolling hills. Lorrie Ann swung around, fearful for a moment of being so alone in the middle of nowhere without her phone.

A blue work-worn truck appeared over the hill. Coming straight at her, the black deer guard on the front looked menacing. The driver slowed down and pulled off the road.

Swallowing, she started praying for it to be a friendly stranger. The door swung open, displaying the Childress quarter-horse logo. Her heartbeat settled. She remembered the Childress family.

From behind the door stepped a walking Hollywood version of the American Cowboy. Tall and lean, his work-faded jeans rode low over slim hips. The dark T-shirt hugged his broad shoulders under a waist-length denim jacket. His fit body looked shaped by hours of working outdoors, instead of designed by a personal trainer. He must be one of the hired ranch hands.

He stepped across the road with confidence and walked in a way that might tempt a girl to give up her plans. Each stride of his long legs moved him closer to her. Her heart flip-flopped. She bit her lip. *Stupid heart.*

She had returned to Clear Water, Texas, to reconnect with God and to refill her spiritual bank, *not* to get tangled up in another relationship. Having her mom's defective gene for picking men, her best option would be to remain male free.

A welcoming smile eased across his face. Lines creased the corners of golden-brown eyes and ran down his well-formed cheeks. One lone dimple appeared on the left side. Her mouth went dry.

"Are you lost?"

His deep Texas drawl washed over her. Lorrie Ann shook her head and searched for words.

"No, but I'm sure that depends on who you ask." A nervous

laugh ran away from her lips. She looked at the ground. *Ugh, let me count the ways to sound like an idiot.* Raising her gaze, she flashed her best smile. In California it never failed her.

Instead, he glanced off into the pasture, at the cows. "Is that your car up ahead?"

She sighed. Apparently, Texas cowboys were a completely different breed from the men she had been working with in Los Angeles.

"Yeah, I ran out of gas."

Bringing his gaze back to her, he looked puzzled. "Town is about eight miles that way." His long fingers pointed in the opposite direction she faced.

"I know, but my phone is somewhere over here." She waved toward the pasture, and her collection of bracelets jingled.

On cue, the phone rang somewhere on the other side of the barbed-wire fence. At least Brent was good for something. "Oh, it still works." She tried to climb between two strands of wire, but a barb snagged her long silk shirt, and her sunglasses hit the ground. When she turned to free the blouse, the top wire caught her hat, causing her hair to fall forward. The thick waves covered her face, blinding her.

"Hold still." The cowboy's voice emitted assurance. Gently his hands freed the corner of her shirt and held the wires farther apart so she could easily step through.

When she stood on the other side, she pushed her hair back. She reached for her oversize shades and shoved them over her eyes. Ouch! She'd forgotten the bruise. Her skin throbbed with a dull ache.

"Are you sure you're okay?" He leaned over the fence, handing her the hat.

Lorrie Ann didn't like the look she read in the cowboy's eyes. At best, it was concern, at worst, pity. Her nails cut into her palms. She hated pity.

"Anyone I can call for you?"

"No, no. Really, as soon as I get my phone, I'm good."

He turned that devastating smile back on her. "How your phone ended up in a cow pasture is bound to be an interesting story." He held his hand out to her, the fence still between them. "I'm John Levi."

The phone sounded off again. Forgetting his hand, she spun around to locate the device. In a tall clump of gold grass, it vibrated. "I found it!" She lifted it high.

He smiled. "Now we just need to get you some gas, and you'll be on your way. Where're you headed?"

"Can you believe my destination is Clear Water?"

Lorrie Ann smiled back at him, a genuine smile this time. It felt good. The past couple years anything real had been hard to find, especially any type of happiness or joy.

"Come on." He chuckled. "Let's get you back on this side of the fence before the herd gets too curious." He stepped on the bottom wire and held the top one up, leaving a large opening.

"Thanks." With one hand on her hat, she stepped through without a problem this time.

"I'll drive you to your car. I have some gas in a can in the back. Not sure your boots could make it down the hill." She had forgotten cowboys always stayed prepared for anything. He held out his arm, like a gentleman from an old movie.

Her fingers wrapped around his denim sleeve. Masculine strength seeped through the sturdy material, warming her skin. "Thank you for helping." Her shoulders rose and fell with a heavy sigh. "I can't believe I ran out of gas this close to arriving home."

"Home? You're a local?" A deep chuckle rumbled from his chest. "I should know better than to judge by appearances or license plates."

"Oh, I'm probably everything you thought. I'm sure if you ask anyone in town, they'll give you all the gory details."

"In order to ask them, I'd have to know your name."

She looked up at him, assessing his expression. "Hmm... that's true." Fear of what they would say tightened her muscles. She had left town in a swirl of lies started by the homecoming queen.

He waited a moment with eyebrows lifted. He finally grinned and closed her door. The cowboy walked around to the driver's side. Climbing into the cab, he continued to grin.

His eyes stayed focused ahead as he eased them back onto the road. "So what brings you back to Clear Water?"

"My aunt. Maggie Schultz."

"You're Maggie's niece, Lorrie Ann Ortega? She didn't say anything about you coming home."

She shouldn't be surprised he knew her. Her aunt volunteered on about every committee in the small town and had always helped anyone that needed something, including her. "She doesn't know."

"She's going to be thrilled."

Lorrie played with the rip in her shirt. He obviously didn't know the whole story. "I'm not so sure about that. It's been a long time."

"She's been waiting for you." He flashed her a quick glance accompanied by a grin. "Trust me. She'll be very excited to see you."

"How do you know her?"

He gave a casual shrug and smiled. "We're at the same church."

The big truck pulled up behind her small BMW. "Go open your tank. I'll get the gas." With a quick motion, he jumped out of the cab and went to the bed of his truck.

Leaping down from the side step, Lorrie Ann made her way to the silver BMW. She glanced into her car and cringed. With the top tucked away on her convertible, he would see the mess she had made in her twenty-five-hour run from California—the candy wrappers, huge plastic cups and haphazard packing that littered the backseat.

Yeah, it pretty much represented her life with Brent in L.A., all pretty and shiny on the outside and chaos on the inside. Now with no gas, the expensive machine sat on the side of the road, useless.

She leaned inside and picked up the Bible. The handwritten note from Aunt Maggie stuck out, purple and tattered around the edges. She didn't need to read the words as they were etched in her memory. *Matthew 11:28, Come to me, all you who are weary and burdened, and I will give you rest.*

Those words had brought her back to Texas, to the closest place she had ever called home. She had been working so hard to prove herself, but somewhere along the way she had lost sight of the big picture.

"You have a note from Maggie." He nodded toward her Bible. "Which verse did she send you? I have a full collection."

Unaware he had approached, Lorrie Ann blinked to clear her thoughts. Did Aunt Maggie send these notes to everyone? Not sure how that made her feel, she laid the Bible back in the car. "She's always looking for ways to help."

He nodded. "She's a prayer warrior. We're blessed to have her."

This all felt very surreal. In the world she just left, no one spoke of God and prayer, let alone Bible verses. And if you did, they'd only laugh and make some witty cut-down.

She pulled in a deep breath. "I need to be going. Thanks so much for your help."

"I'll follow you into town. The closest gas station is the mercantile. We can stop there and get you filled up then head out to Bill and Maggie's farm."

"Oh, no. You've done enough."

"It's on my way. I can't look your uncle and aunt in the eye if I don't make sure you're delivered safe and sound." He winked at her. "See you in town." He stepped back and walked to his truck.

Okay, then. Her knight in denim remained on the job. She shouldn't like the idea. Slipping into her car, Lorrie Ann turned the key and pulled back onto the road. With a glance at her rearview mirror, she watched John follow her.

Scolding herself, she muttered, "Remember, Lorrie Ann, your short-term goal is to get your life back in order and get back to work. A boyfriend's not even on the long-term list."

John Levi turned on the radio. Music he had shut out five years ago filled the cabin of his truck. His fingers tipped the guitar pick hanging from the rearview mirror. Carol, his wife, had given it to him when they were still dating. He watched the heart she had drawn on it swing back and forth. It was the only piece of his music career he kept after her death. The pick reminded him of what he had taken for granted.

The sporty car in front of him pulled out, and he followed. Lorrie Ann Ortega was a surprise, and any pull he felt had to do with her needing help. Through her aunt and mother, he knew her past, and now he saw the wounded look in her eyes. She needed encouragement and support. He could do that for her.

He tapped his fingers along the cracked steering wheel.

Holding the phone in her hand, Lorrie Ann wavered calling Aunt Maggie. What if she didn't want her? Her mother hadn't wanted her. Now that she was an adult, her aunt and uncle had no responsibility to help her.

As she came into town, she eased on the brake. A burst of purple and silver stretched across Main Street and covered every storefront window, each proudly supporting the Fighting Angoras football team.

Homecoming week. The day after graduation, she'd made sure to tell everyone that she would never be back. How ironic that she return the week of the homecoming game. Some rituals never changed. Lorrie smiled. An unexpected comfort washed over her. Not a single fast-food or chain-store logo cluttered the skyline.

Her phone vibrated. With clenched teeth, she battled the urge to throw the phone out of the car again. She imagined running over it until nothing but dust clung to her tires.

She wanted to leave everything in Los Angeles behind, long enough to figure out her life, anyway. The band had taken the holidays off. Could she develop a new-life action plan in less than four weeks?

Pulling next to the aged gas pumps, Lorrie Ann pushed the button to roll the top back over the car. She took a deep breath, slid out of the car and straightened her spine.

Her hands shook slightly as she adjusted the oversize shades. Lorrie Ann ran a manicured finger over the convertible top of her Z4 BMW. Definitely not the hand-me-down Dodge she had driven away in as a scared teenager.

She took a slow surveillance of the single-street town. A group of old ranchers still sat in front of the feed store. Their never-ending game of dominoes was as much a part of the landscape as the giant oaks.

John parked his truck on the other side of her. "Here, let me fill her up for you."

She was not used to men offering to do things for her unless they wanted something. It made her a bit uncomfortable. She noticed new construction at the end of the street, an unheard-of occurrence in Clear Water. She gestured to the site, causing her bracelets to jingle. "What's being built? Looks like a regular building boom for Clear Water."

He nodded and smiled at her as he held the gas nozzle to her car. "The churches have banded together to build a new youth building."

A gleam came to his eyes, reminding her of a proud parent. Bringing his gaze back to hers, he continued, "There's still some fundraising that needs to be done, but enough has been raised to get the building started."

"Wow, I'm impressed." She cut a glance toward him again. He turned his gaze on her, started to say something and then looked away.

The silence stretched and got awkward. She bit her lip. *Say something, girl.*

"Um…so are you involved in the project?"

"It's my goal to see it done before summer." Nodding, he stepped back and replaced the nozzle. "Well, your steed is fed. I'll walk you to the store."

She couldn't hold in the giggle. Did she just actually giggle? Lorrie Ann took a moment to savor the joy.

"Thank you." She slid a glance to the old ranchers, now openly staring at her and the cowboy. She waved at them. "Hi, boys." Swinging back to her knight in faded denim, she winked. "Think they appreciated the show?"

He laughed. A real laugh not measured or managed.

"They enjoy anything new to talk about. Are you good? I could wait."

"No, I'm fine. I need to pick up a few items, then I'll make my escape to the pecan farm." Yep, she had become very skilled at running. "Thank you for the escort."

He looked right into her eyes, and for a second she forgot to breathe. She had the sensation he saw past the makeup and fashion to the real her.

"It's a true pleasure meeting you, Lorrie Ann Ortega. Welcome back." He tipped his hat and pulled open one of the glass double doors to the mercantile for her. A little bell made a sweet musical sound.

He gave her one last wink. "I'm sure we'll see each other again. Can't hide in a town this small."

The door closed, and she turned and watched through the large storefront windows as he walked away. Once he disappeared from sight, she noticed the flyers in an array of colors taped everywhere, announcing cabins for rent, hunting leases available and horses for sale. Well, she was back.

A loud squeal filled the air followed by a high-pitched voice. "L.A.? Lorrie Ann. Oh, my, it is you!"

Lorrie Ann cringed at her old nickname. No one had called her L.A. for years. She found herself ambushed in a tight hug by a tall woman with big blond hair. Knocked off balance, Lorrie Ann grabbed the girl's arms. A death grip kept her from moving back. The overzealous greeter yelled over her shoulder, "Vickie, hurry out here. L.A. is back in Clear Water!"

"Katy? Katy Norton?" Relief flooded Lorrie as she greeted one of the few girls she trusted from high school.

"I didn't recognize you till you came in. You sure look fancy. I hear you hang with rock stars now. Your aunt says you're getting married to the drummer of Burn White." Katy leaned back, but her hands remained clasped around Lorrie's forearm. "Maggie didn't say anything about you coming for a visit."

"She doesn't know. How are you?" Lorrie Ann glanced around the grocery store. From the hundred-year-old wooden floor to the meat counter in the back, all appeared the same as it did in her memories. "You work at the mercantile?"

"I married Rhody. We manage the store for his parents now."

"You married Rhody Buchanan?" Lorrie Ann forced her eyebrows back down. "He picked on you in high school."

Katy smirked and playfully slapped Lorrie Ann on the shoulder. "Well, I came to find out it was just his way of flirting. We have four boys now."

"You and Rhody have four kids…together?" Her forehead went up again.

Before Katy could answer, Vickie Lawson, the conductor of Lorrie Ann's high-school nightmare, ambled from the deer-corn aisle.

"Well, well, well, if it isn't big-city girl L.A." Vickie's

stare slowly moved up and down. "Thought you were never coming back to our town."

"Honestly, I'm as surprised as you are to find myself here. I came to visit Aunt Maggie for the holidays." Lorrie Ann's gaze darted around the store.

Katy hugged her again. "She's been waiting for you. We've all prayed for you to come home." She threw her arms wide. "And lookie, you're here, an answered prayer. You'll have to tell me all about your exciting adventures in L.A." Katy sighed.

Lorrie Ann could hear the expectation of glamorous stories about life in Los Angeles.

Vickie crossed her arms and leaned against the counter, face pulled tight. "Where's your boyfriend? Waitin' in the car? Probably thinks he's too good for the likes of us."

Lorrie Ann drew a deep breath and smiled the smile she used to close deals with in L.A. "No, he's not here. We broke up." She turned to Katy with a genuine smile. "Once I get settled, we can have lunch or something."

"Ooh, just like in the movies!" Katy tilted her head. "Will you be at church for our Wednesday-night prayer meeting?" She nudged Lorrie Ann's shoulder. "Looks like you already know Pastor John."

A frown replaced the smile when the word *pastor* sank into Lorrie Ann's brain. Only one other person had spoken to her. That good-looking cowboy couldn't have been a…

"That cowboy is a preacher?" Her jaw dropped, and she closed her eyes. Horror stomped out the shock. She had flirted with a man of God.

Katy's smile went wider as her eyes sparkled. "Yes! He seemed to really like you."

Vickie gave a loud snort and narrowed her glare. "You've always tried taking men who aren't yours. He *will* see right through you."

Katy punched Vickie's arm and laughed. "Oh, stop it!

Lorrie Ann just got into town. We don't need to bring up what happened in the past. Anyway, Pastor John has not dated anyone since the horrible accident five years ago. I think it's about time he left his daughters at home and went out for some fun."

"Whatever." With a shrug, Vickie turned and walked to the back of the store.

Lorrie Ann's chin went up. No longer was she the pathetic girl abandoned by her mother. Now she made big deals and managed bands in her daily life. She controlled her destiny. Not some…

A warm hand on her arm brought her around.

"Don't let her get under your skin. She's always been jealous of you." Katy waved her hand in the air and lowered her voice. "And since the divorce, she's just gotten downright bitter. She should have never married Tommy. Poor thing, her life is a mess right now. Let's get your stuff so you can go home."

Katy's soft gaze brought a knot to Lorrie Ann's throat. Well, she could relate to a messy life. "I always thought her and Jake were an item. She hated my friendship with him."

"Yeah, now they are both back in town and avoiding each other—sad, really." Katy shook her head. "Come on. Let's get your things so you can surprise Maggie."

Purchases in hand, Lorrie Ann stepped out of the store and spotted the Ford truck still parked outside the mercantile. She groaned. Less than thirty minutes in town, and she had already been flirting with the town pastor right on Main Street. The gossips would have a field day with that tidbit.

Chapter Two

"Aunt Maggie? It's—"

"Oh, *mija,* it's so good to hear from you!" A slight pause came through the line. "Is everything okay?"

The love and concern in the older woman's voice wrapped itself around Lorrie Ann's heart. Eyes closed briefly, she eased a smile across her face.

"Yeah, I'm good. I'm actually in Clear Water heading to the farm." As the silence lingered, her stomach knotted.

"What? Oh, my, Lorrie Ann Ortega! What do you mean you're in Clear Water? Why are you just now calling me?" Lorrie could almost hear her aunt's thoughts processing. "Oh, sweetheart, what happened?"

"Nothing.... I just need a place to rest, get my thoughts together. Is it okay that I came to the farm? I don't know Mom's latest location." Nerves hit her stomach hard. "It's just for a couple weeks while I figure things out. I can rent one of the cabins."

"You hush about paying. This is your home. Your room's always ready for you."

Lorrie pulled in her lips and bit down. The need to cry burned her eyes. She pulled a deep breath through her nose before she dared speak again. "Thank you, Aunt Maggie. I'm at Second Crossing now, so I'll—"

A deer darted across the road. Her phone slid to the floorboard as she grabbed the steering wheel with both hands. Hitting the brake, she pulled her car to the side of the road.

The deer's hooves slid on the pavement, fighting to regain control. The white of the doe's eyes flashed, and in a frenzied twist it turned back the way it had come and ran behind her.

In Lorrie Ann's rearview mirror, she tracked the animal as it scurried right in front of a yellow Jeep. Eyes wide, Lorrie Ann watched the events as if in slow motion. Horror filled her mind as the deer collided with the grille of the oncoming vehicle. The deer flew over the hood into the windshield, and the Jeep lost control. It slid in the loose gravel and rolled toward the river. Frozen in her seat, Lorrie Ann stared as a group of cedar trees stopped the rolling car.

"Lorrie! Lorrie Ann, answer me!" Her aunt's frantic voice brought her back to herself. White fingers had a death grip around the leather of her steering wheel. As she reached for the phone between her feet, her hands shook. She took a deep breath. The dark shades fell to the floorboard, and she didn't bother picking them up.

"I'm here. I'm fine, but there's been an accident. I have to call 911." Without waiting to hear her aunt's response, she ended the call and hit the emergency button. She stepped out of her car and jogged along the shoulder of the road, her heels clicking across the asphalt. Breath held tight, she approached the flipped vehicle. When she heard crying, relief eased her muscles a small bit, proof of life.

She knelt to look in the cab, her heart pounding at the thought of what she might see. A young girl hung upside down by her seat belt in the backseat.

A sob muffled her words. "Rachel! Rachel!"

Her weeping broke Lorrie's heart. "Sweetheart, my name's Lorrie Ann. I called the ambulance."

The voice on the line demanded her attention, asking for details. "There has been a car accident at Second Crossing.

Oh, I'm Lorrie Ann Ortega. There's a girl about five or six in the backseat. She is awake and suspended by her seat belt."

Lorrie scanned the cab, noticing two more girls up front. Broken glass covered the roof, but the roll bars had done their job and created a pocket for them.

The passenger in the front seat appeared to be around ten or twelve. "There are two girls in the front, both strapped in their seats. The driver has blood on her face. She looks unconscious." A deep sigh of relief escaped. "But breathing."

The young girl in front started twisting against her shoulder strap. "Celeste? Celeste, where are you?" A frantic tone edged her voice.

"Rachel! I'm…I'm scared." The smaller one in the backseat reached forward.

"Don't be scared. Stop crying! It won't help." Her voice sounded more mature than her age.

Lorrie Ann couldn't help being impressed. "Girls, help is on the way. Are you sisters?" Their matching ponytails bobbed as they nodded their heads. "It's Rachel and Celeste, right?"

"Yes." The older girl in the front spoke, moving both hands to rub at her face. "Amy's our babysitter. Oh, Daddy's going to be so mad."

"I'm sure your father just wants you safe."

"Oh! My leg is stuck. I can't move it." Rachel sounded calm, though her voice pitched higher at the last word.

Lorrie Ann narrowed her gaze on Rachel's right leg surrounded by metal. It looked as if a piece of the engine had pushed through.

The driver groaned.

"Amy, Amy, wake up!" Rachel reached across and touched her shoulder.

"What happened?" Amy pushed back her hair. "Oh, no!" She sucked in deep breaths, and her eyes went wide. "Rachel?

Celeste? Please, please tell me you're all right!" She cried out in pain, hugging herself and moaning.

"Easy. Don't hurt yourself." Lorrie Ann pressed a hand to the older girl's shoulder. "I hear the sirens. Help's almost here. Just hang on, girls, and try to stay still."

Lorrie Ann turned from the crumbled metal and watched as an ambulance arrived.

A state trooper pulled in from the other direction. He quickly stepped from his car and made his way to the wreckage. Lorrie Ann squinted against the sun to get a better look at him and then hung her head.

He hunched next to her, scanning the inside of the car. "Hang tight, Amy. Girls, we'll have you out soon." He turned until she saw her reflection in his aviators. "Lorrie Ann Ortega? What in the world are you doing here?"

She stared into the face of another ghost from her past. Even with the dark shades masking most of his face, she knew who hovered over her.

"Jake Torres, I'm trying to help three scared girls here."

He nodded. Bracing a hand on the door as he peered back inside, he spoke again, his voice softened. "We're here to help you girls. So breathe and stay calm."

He glanced back at Lorrie Ann over his shoulder. "Girl, you sure know how to make an entrance back to town."

Making his way to the post office, John could not stop the urge to whistle a sweet tune as he waved to the cars slowly passing by. The plans for his day had fallen apart when Dub called, needing help with a renegade horse.

He smiled, remembering his frustration when the church secretary, JoAnn, called right after with a problem at the construction site. Both unscheduled events put Maggie's niece right in his path.

It had been a long time since he allowed himself to enjoy the company of a female. He should have fully introduced himself, but he suspected the easy camaraderie would have ended. As soon as someone found out he was a pastor, they started acting differently around him. Ordinarily the attitude didn't bother him, but today, he just wanted to be a normal man getting to know another person. Another person who happened to be a woman.

That thought gave him pause. He tilted his face toward the sky, trying to recall how long it had been. Time had a way of slipping past unnoticed.

The tiny, dark-haired female had boldly gotten his attention. He grinned. Knee-high boots were not his style, but something about her had radiated past her appearance. He shook his head and started walking again. He needed to get back to the task at hand. Guilt roared at him. He had no right to flirt with anyone.

With a quick flip of his wrist, he checked the time. In order to make his lunch date, he had to get in and out of the post office undetected by any well-meaning parishioners.

With a slow pull on the glass door to ensure the bells remained silent, John slipped into the small post office and held his breath. With a swift glance to his left, he found the room clear.

Today he would not break his promise to the girls. He would be home by noon. A grin pulled at the corners of his mouth as he thought of all the whispering and giggling involved in planning a surprise picnic for him. He never seemed to spend enough time with them.

Small-town life had become much more complicated than he'd imagined when he'd accepted the job as senior pastor four years ago.

He pulled the envelopes from the square compartment and gently closed the long brass door to box 1, feeling like a CIA spy behind enemy lines…almost free.

"Oh, Pastor John, what a pleasant surprise. What brings you into the post office so early?"

Caught. For a split second, his shoulders sagged, and he closed his eyes.

"Pastor John? Is everything okay? I have the cranberry-oatmeal cookies you love so much." Postmistress for the past thirty years, Emily Martin spoke around her daily chicken-salad sandwich. "They're in the back."

Relaxing tight muscles, John put on his welcoming smile and glanced down at the tiny woman who made him feel taller than his six-foot frame.

"No, thanks. The girls are waiting for me." He glanced at his escape route. Fondness for the sweet lady won over. "How are you today, Miss Emily?"

"Oh, those babies—that oldest looks just like her momma, poor thing. Well, my sister is pestering me again about Momma's house and my knee is bothering me, which I hope means we'll be getting some rain—the ground's so dry—but other than that, I can't complain." She swallowed her last bite. "It's all in God's hands, right, Pastor John?"

"Yes, it is." John glanced behind Emily again, to the door only five feet away. So close yet so far. "Well, I've got to be going. You have a nice day."

Behind his smile, John gritted his back teeth. Utter defeat consumed him as he watched Elva De La Soto, another elder member of his church, open the door. She rushed in wearing the familiar expression of tragedy on her face.

"Pastor John! I'm so glad you're here. There's been an accident at Second Crossing. It's the Campbell girl's Jeep. Is she babysitting your girls today?"

John ran to his truck and drove toward the pecan farm without a conscious thought. Fear and faith clashed in John's brain. His phone started buzzing. Recalling the phone call about his wife's accident, he froze. He stared at the unfamiliar number. If he didn't answer he could stay ignorant of any bad news. He prayed with every fiber of his being for his girls' safety.

Why had they been in the babysitter's car? They weren't allowed to travel with anyone without his permission. Amy knew his rules. His mind numb and his knuckles gripping the steering wheel, John turned onto Highway 83.

Faith would enable him to handle whatever waited for him. With a firm move, he accepted the call.

"This is John." His own voice sounded foreign.

"Daddy?" a small tentative voice came over the line.

Relief flooded his body, and his hands began to shake. John cleared his dry throat. "Hey, sweet girl. Are you okay?"

"I'm…I'm a little scared, but Rachel told me not to be. The car is upside down. A deer ran into us. Ms. Amy and Rachel are in the ambulance. Rachel told me not to cry, and Lorrie Ann said everything'll be okay." She sniffled. "Daddy, please come get me."

Amy's yellow Jeep came into view. He swallowed back the bile that rose from his stomach. Reality and memories tangled in his vision. Flashes of his wife's crumbled silver Focus clouded his eyesight. The accident had been his fault. Shaking his head, he forced himself to focus on today.

All four wheels faced the clear sky. The driver's side was smashed against a cedar break. The trees had stopped the Jeep's free fall into the river below. At the sight, his body stiffened; he could no longer feel his limbs.

His two little girls had been in that jumbled piece of metal.

John pulled his truck to an abrupt stop on the side of the highway, the loose gravel crunching under his tires. His gaze scanned the area.

The trooper's red and blue lights reflected over the people starting to mill around the crushed car. His six-year-old daughter sat on the front seat of a little BMW, her bare feet dangling in front of Lorrie Ann.

His throat closed up, and for a minute, he couldn't breathe. *Thank You, God! Thank You!*

"I'm right behind you, baby. I'm here. I'm going to hang up now, okay?"

His youngest daughter's head whipped around, searching for him. Before his boots left the old truck, she had started running to him. In a few strides, he had her pulled up close against his heart.

Her thin arms tightened around his neck, threatening to cut off his air. One hand cradled the back of her head; the other scooped up her bottom. Her legs wrapped around his torso.

"Hey, monkey. It's all right. I'm here. I've got you." He whispered into her ear, taking in the smell of her apple shampoo. He closed his eyes and for a moment focused on her heartbeat. The warmth of her tiny body absorbed into his.

Thank You, God.

He opened his eyes and found Lorrie Ann staring up at him.

"Hello again." She reached out and patted Celeste's back. "I was first on the scene. Amy and Rachel are with the EMTs. They'll be fine—just a bit more banged up." Her voice remained calm, and the softness in her eyes soothed him with the compassion he saw.

He glanced to the open doors of the ambulance. Fear slammed its way through his gut. Celeste wiggled under his tightened grip. He closed his eyes, sent a quick prayer and relaxed his muscles.

"You can take Celeste with you. I promise it's not bad." Her smile reassured him she understood his hesitation of taking Celeste to the ambulance.

What she couldn't see? The images flashing in his mind of his wife's accident. He swallowed hard and pressed his lips against Celeste's forehead. With another prayer, he hurried across the street to his oldest daughter while carting his six-year-old on his hip.

"Rachel?" He poked his head around the door only to find Amy, his seventeen-year-old babysitter, on the stretcher. "Hello, Amy."

She wouldn't meet his gaze. "Pastor Levi, I'm so sorry. I know I wasn't supposed to take them, but they wanted apples for the chicken salad. They said it was your favorite. I'm so sorry."

"I just want y'all to be safe."

From the far side, he heard voices.

"Daddy? Are you there?" Ducking around the ambulance, he found Rachel. His stress lightened a bit at the sight of Brenda Castillo, in her blue EMT uniform, bent over his daughter's leg.

"Hello, Pastor John." Brenda smiled at Rachel. "See, I told you he would get here before we left."

"Daddy, I'm so sorry." Huge tears spilled out of her eyes. "I'm so sorry."

His chest clenched at the sight. "Oh, princess, there's nothing for you to apologize for. It was an accident." He went to bend down, but with Celeste still in his arms, he almost lost his balance.

"Here, let me help." The soft voice surprised him.

Lorrie Ann had followed them over. Before he could do anything, a pink zebra-print golf cart drew everyone's attention as it charged onto the highway. Dust flew as the small woman, Margarita Schultz, set a determined course straight at them.

"Aunt Maggie!" his daughters and Lorrie Ann yelled as one voice.

The cart threw pebbles as it slid to a stop. Without slowing down, Maggie jumped from the seat. Short black-and-silver-streaked hair flew around her face. Large dark eyes flashed with worry as she hurried over. "What is going on here, *mija?* You scared me to death with that call, young lady." She looked around, and her hand went to her chest. "Oh, no,

Amy's Jeep is…" She went to her heels beside Rachel. "Oh, *mija,* are you all right?" She glanced at Brenda and then to John. "Is she going to be all right?"

"Her leg needs to be x-rayed." Brenda spoke to John. "We have it stabilized. You can take Rachel to the hospital yourself. Steve and I are taking Amy to Uvalde."

Maggie turned back to John. "You take Rachel." She put a hand out to rub the slim back of John's youngest daughter. "We'll take care of Celeste. You won't feel right until you have Rachel all safe and sound. I'll start the prayer chain."

"Are you sure, Maggie?" Torn, he pushed his daughter's loose curls behind her ear, hesitating. "Maybe I should take Celeste with me."

"You don't know how long you'll be there. We'll make sure she eats lunch. I'd get you something to eat, too, but I know you won't touch a thing until you see for yourself Rachel is fine. So go on with you."

"Thank you, Maggie." With a finger under her little pointed chin, John lifted his tiny daughter's face up to his. "Do you want to stay with Aunt Maggie?"

She nodded slowly and, to his surprise, reached for Lorrie Ann. Maggie's niece extended her arms, pulling the little precious body from him. He reluctantly let her go.

In truth, he wanted to hold on to her forever, but he needed to get to Rachel and focus on her. "Lorrie Ann, thanks for being here and staying with them."

"I'm glad I could help."

Her smile held him mesmerized for a moment, until he heard Maggie's gasp. She had noticed the bruise under Lorrie Ann's eye.

"Were you hurt, too?"

"No. It's just a bump. Go on," she said to him. "You need to get Rachel to the doctor."

As a pastor, he had gotten good at spotting a guilty face, and Lorrie Ann's screamed guilt as she sliced a look back from him to her aunt. They both knew the bruise had been there before the accident.

With a last kiss on Celeste's forehead, he promised to return soon.

Lorrie Ann watched as John carried his injured daughter across the street. Her heart ached at the careful tenderness he used to settle her in the cab of his old Ford.

She wondered what it felt like to be cherished that way. With a shake of her head, she forced her attention back to the child and Aunt Maggie. "Well, ladies, ready to go to the house?"

"I want to ride in the zebra car."

"No, you go on with Lorrie Ann. I'm going to speak to a few people." Maggie turned and cut off a small crowd heading their way, sacrificing herself to the persistent string of questions. Lorrie Ann gratefully dodged the mob and hurried to her BMW.

She buckled her new friend in and headed for the ranch house up the hill.

"Do you live close by, Celeste?"

Celeste twisted and stretched from her seat belt, looking out the window. Her blond curls bounced with each bob of her head.

"Yes, ma'am, we live in the big cabin there—the one behind Aunt Maggie's house." She pointed and turned back to Lorrie with a grin.

Lorrie fought the urge to bang her head against the steering wheel. Of course they did. Where else would he live, other than the cabin a few steps from her aunt's back door?

Chapter Three

Lorrie Ann paused at the wrought-iron gate that led to the terra-cotta-paved courtyard. Wisteria and roses climbed the white stucco walls. The large ranch house rambled off both sides of the patio. Lorrie Ann smiled at the turquoise door.

All the hours and years she'd spent waiting for her mother to come back rushed in and filled her mind.

"Are we waiting for Aunt Maggie?"

The child's voice pulled her back to the present. She smiled down at the rumpled-looking doll and took the small hand in hers.

"No, just caught up in some memories." Pulling air through her nose and slowly releasing her breath, she took one step forward. "Let's go to the kitchen door. I bet she has something we can heat up for lunch."

Obviously familiar with the home, Celeste headed to the breezeway. The traffic-worn stones gave testimony that family and friends went straight to the back door.

Stepping into the kitchen, Lorrie Ann had the unexpected urge to cry. Spices from all the meals cooked over the years lingered in the air. The clay bean pot and flat cast-iron griddle sat on the old white stove.

"Did you live here when you were a little girl?" Celeste

asked as she twirled in the middle of the large open kitchen. "I want tortillas. Do you think she has some *papas?*"

"Now, that is a word I have not heard in a while." Lorrie Ann opened the refrigerator door and dug around until she found an old margarine tub with cubed potatoes that had been panfried. "Here we go—*papas!*"

"And tortillas!" Celeste held a wicker basket of tortillas like a trophy. "But I'm not allowed to touch the stove."

Lorrie Ann turned on the burner and adjusted the flame.

"After school, my cousin, Yolanda, and I would race in here to fight over the first tortilla." Maggie's daughter always argued that since she was younger by four years and it was her mother who made them that she should get the first one.

At the counter that separated the kitchen from the dining room, Celeste jumped on a stool and started spinning in circles. "Is Aunt Maggie your real aunt? Did your mom and dad live here, too?"

"Maggie is my mom's older sister. My mom traveled, so I just stayed here." The story slipped from her lips naturally as she flipped the tortilla.

"What about your dad?" The child spun the chair in the opposite direction.

"My father?" A good question her mother never answered. "Um…well. He's gone."

"He's dead?"

Lorrie Ann gasped. "Oh, no." What had she done? "Oh, oh, no. I mean…I don't know. No, uh…" How did she get out of this?

"You don't know? I'll ask Daddy to pray for him. Rachel says he has the most important job in the world."

Lorrie Ann scooped the potatoes into the warm tortilla. She glanced at the door. "Aunt Maggie should be here any minute." With plate in hand, she turned away from the stove to face the child.

Celeste's head popped up over a pyramid made of red cups. Her tongue stuck out between rows of tiny white teeth.

Lorrie Ann froze. "Oh, my…you…um…you need to sit down."

"I just need to add the last guard to my castle." She balanced the spoon against the side of the top cup, but as she pulled away, the whole structure collapsed.

Heart in her throat, Lorrie Ann dropped the plate on the counter and rushed to grab Celeste before she fell. "I think it would be better if you didn't stand on a swivel chair." With a heavy sigh, she started picking up the cups.

Celeste joined her. "I'm sorry, Miss Lorrie Ann. My sister says I need to learn to sit still." Her voice sounded subdued.

With a forced smile, she faced the little girl. "No harm done." She patted her on the head. "It's okay, rug rat." They put the last cup back on the counter. "See, everything's back in place and nothing broken. But I would suggest not standing on moving chairs." She patted the seat. "Cool tower, by the way."

"Thanks." The smile beamed again.

"Here you go. Time to eat." She scanned her brain for a safe topic. "I think I saw grapes. Do you want some?" She went back to the refrigerator and pulled out a clear bag full of the fruit. While washing them, she glanced out the big picture window, hoping to see her aunt. She sighed at the empty driveway and tore off a small bunch of grapes for Celeste.

"Oh, I can't eat whole grapes. Daddy says they have to be cut in half so I don't choke. Hot dogs, too." She tossed a cubed potato in her mouth. "Why do they call the purple crayon *grape* when grapes are green? Will you please cut them? Daddy won't let me use a knife."

"Sure." She pulled a small knife from the same drawer they had been in twelve years ago.

"I tell Daddy that only babies eat cut grapes, but he says I'll always be his baby." She stuck out her tongue and scrunched her little nose.

"In Los Angeles, cut grapes are gourmet food. I only eat sliced grapes myself." She pulled a white plastic knife from the drawer and handed it over to Celeste. "Here, you can use a plastic knife."

Together they sliced the grapes. Lorrie Ann tossed one up to catch in her mouth, but it bounced off her chin, causing the sweetest giggle to come from the other side of the counter. She closed one eye and looked at the little girl with the other. "Hey! Are you laughing at me?"

Celeste sat up straight. Her ponytail swung with the shake of her head while her shoulders trembled as she failed to hold down her laughter.

Both turned at the sound of the screen door opening.

"Aunt Maggie, look! Miss Lorrie Ann taught me how to make gourmet grapes."

"She has always been very creative." She smiled at them then headed to the red wall phone. "Give me a minute. I need to start the prayer chain and call your grandpa."

"He's at the five hundred pasture today, Aunt Maggie."

Maggie ran her finger down a list of names. "Well, then, I'll just leave him a message." She pushed the buttons on the phone. Bare spots on the twisted ten-foot cord exposed colored cables.

Lorrie Ann smiled. "Do you ever think about getting a cordless?"

"Oh, Yolanda bought me one of those, but I lose it all the time. This one works just fine." As she listened to the rings on the other end, she glanced around the kitchen. "Where'd Celeste go?"

With a gasp, Lorrie Ann turned to the empty chair the little girl had been sitting on, and her heart froze in her chest. How did she lose one little person? "Celeste?"

She moved through the large archway that led to the family room. "Celeste?" Behind her, she heard muffled giggling. Shooting her aunt a questioning look, she only received a smile and shrug. Aunt Maggie turned to finish her phone call.

So, she was on her own again with the small creature. "Celeste, where are you?" She started scanning the floor and under the counter.

Huddled in a ball under the ten-foot pine table, Celeste giggled again.

Lorrie Ann went to the floor. "May I ask why you're hiding in the chair legs?"

"I'm a rabbit and this is my home."

"How about a movie?" Aunt Maggie asked from across the room.

Celeste wiggled her nose. "Okay." She started hopping out then stopped. "You'll stay with me?"

The same golden-brown eyes Lorrie Ann had looked into this morning pierced her heart. What would it be like to see your own features in a child? She doubted she'd ever know.

"Sure."

Less than fifteen minutes into some princess movie, Celeste fell asleep, curled up like a kitten with her head resting on Lorrie Ann's thigh. She closed her eyes and tilted her head back on the overstuffed leather sofa.

Aunt Maggie walked into the living room. "I figured she'd go to sleep." One click of the remote and the princess's song went silent. "Now, Lorrie Ann Ortega, you will tell me what happened that brought you home."

Lorrie Ann kept her eyes closed and wondered how long she could fake sleep.

"I know you aren't asleep."

Apparently less than a minute. With a heavy sigh, she opened her eyes.

"I needed to get away. Once I was on IH 10, coming here just felt right." She rubbed her arms and studied the sleeping child in her lap. "I really don't want to talk about it right now.

I have the holidays off, so here I am. After Christmas I'll go back to L.A. recharged and ready to take on the world again."

"Is it your fiancé?" Her aunt's voice turned quiet. "Does it have anything to do with that bruise?"

"Now that I'm here I'm fine." *As long as I don't become my mother.* "You don't need to worry about Brent. That's definitely off, no regrets, no maybes about it. We are over."

"Okay, then." She reached over and picked up her quilting hoop. "This is your home. I'm glad you're here." She placed her purple reading glasses low on her nose and contemplated the stitching in her hands. "We can throw a party."

Lorrie Ann groaned and ran her hands through her hair. Ugh, she needed a shower. She rested her head on the back of the sofa. "There are people who won't be happy I'm back." The one thing she regretted most was bringing shame to Aunt Maggie and Uncle Billy. "You know I didn't leave on the best of terms."

Aunt Maggie slipped off her glasses and moved to sit next to Lorrie Ann. Reaching past Celeste, she put her hand on Lorrie Ann's shoulder. "*Mija,* I have prayed every day that God brings you back to your family." A soft smile eased its way across her milk-chocolate skin. She pushed a piece of hair away from Lorrie Ann's face. "Let the petty high-school drama go."

At her aunt's soft touch, Lorrie Ann felt like a little girl again.

"When you're ready, you can talk to me." She gently squeezed her shoulder. "But know this…you sitting here is an answer to many, many prayers."

Uncomfortable with the love in her aunt's gaze, Lorrie Ann turned her head and closed her eyes to block the feelings of guilt. Instead, she focused on the heartbeat of the sleeping child in her lap.

Maggie stood and placed her quilting hoop back in the

basket. "I need to call around to make sure Amy's parents have meals."

Lorrie Ann relaxed and closed her eyes again but couldn't shut off her brain.

Her hand moved to stroke the silky blond hair of the little person in her lap. She smiled, thinking of Celeste's father.

Her gaze fell across the family pictures on the bookshelf. Smiling faces of her many aunts and uncles along with all the cousins crowded together in mismatched frames. She lingered over the only picture of her with her mother. Blue-and-purple icing smeared on both their faces at her tenth birthday, the last birthday she'd spent with her mom. Happiness filled the face of the little girl she had been, thinking her mother would stay.

She realized returning to the farm, she wanted to find the family she never really knew and the only place she had felt God.

The image of John holding his daughters crossed her mind and melted her heart. What would it have been like to have that kind of father? Her mother had refused to say her father's name. Lorrie Ann had eventually stopped asking.

She watched her manicured nail make little circles on Celeste's shirt. John's life reflected God. Hers? Not so much.

She rested her cheek on her other hand supported by the arm of the sofa. Even though she shouldn't want to see more of his dream-changing smiles, she found herself listening for an old blue truck's tires on the gravel driveway.

Chapter Four

John turned the key and shut the engine off. Sitting in the silence, he watched the full moon reflect over the river below. Rachel had fallen asleep on the way home, her leg now in a black stabilizer from ankle to the top of her thigh. In a few days when the swelling went down, he'd have to take her back for the cast. Her apologies had run nonstop. Several times, he reassured her it would be fine, but his preteen seemed to pick up his doubts.

All the problems bounced around his brain. With his eyes closed, he pressed his forehead against the cracked steering wheel.

"God, I know worry is a sin. Please show me how I can be the pastor people need and the father my girls deserve."

The to-do list started clicking off in his head. The youth building still needed funds, his house sat gutted and Dub needed help with the ranch. The big annual Christmas pageant loomed around the corner, with no one to direct it. He sighed. Now Rachel required extra help, and his babysitter, Amy, was out while she recovered.

Deep in thought, he jumped when a hand pounded on his window. He opened the door, but before he could move, Celeste had climbed into his lap. Her small hands framed his face.

"Hello, Daddy."

He smiled and covered her precious fingers with his hands. "Hey, monkey. How are you?" He turned to Lorrie Ann, Celeste's late-night escort, and grinned. Was it only this morning they'd first met? "Did she cause you any problems?"

She shook her head. "No, we had fun."

"Daddy, I was good, and Miss Lorrie Ann let me use a knife."

He shot a heated glare to the woman who had kept creeping into his mind all day. "You let a five-year-old use a *knife?*"

"No, no, it was a plastic knife. You know, the small picnic ones."

"Daddy, I'm six now. I turned six at the football game. I could cut my own grapes." She rested her head on his shoulder, facing her sister. "What's wrong with her leg?"

"It's broken. I need to get her into the house."

"Come here, rug rat. Let your dad out of the truck, and we can get you all settled in the cabin."

His daughter giggled as she reached for Lorrie Ann's hand.

"She calls me rug rat, Daddy, because they're cute, real smart and are always moving around." She swung her arm back and forth. "Right, Miss Lorrie Ann?"

"Yes, ma'am." Lorrie Ann brought her face back to his. "Aunt Maggie sent some dinner over." With her free hand, she lifted a foil-covered plate.

Celeste led Lorrie Ann toward the porch. The security light automatically flooded the area as they reached the steps.

"It's unlocked." They went inside as he made his way around the truck feeling much older than his thirty-one years.

He opened the passenger door and slipped his arms under Rachel. Careful of her leg, he pulled her to him. She was eleven now. For a moment, he pulled her closer and closed his eyes. When was the last time he had carried her from the car? So many moments in life just slipped past without thought or fanfare.

Headlights came up the driveway and parked behind his truck. His head slumped for a minute as he hoped it was not some concerned member of his congregation, but then he prayed for forgiveness and patience.

"Are our girls all right?"

Relief relaxed his shoulders as his father-in-law's baritone voice came from the dark. He should have known a phone call wouldn't be enough.

"Hey, Dub. Celeste doesn't have a scratch on her. Rachel has a broken leg. Amy has the most injuries, with a broken collarbone and concussion. They kept her overnight."

"Daddy?" Rachel's head lifted.

"Hey, sweetheart, we're home. And look, Grandpa's here."

"Hi, Grandpa." Her head went back to his chest.

Dub followed, carrying the silver crutches and closing all the doors behind them.

John scanned the open living room and kitchen area. He grimaced at the shoes, books and crayons scattered on the area rug. The kitchen had a stack of dirty dishes in the sink, and it looked as if the girls had been making sandwiches before they left for town.

"Grandpa!" Celeste flew down the wrought-iron spiral staircase.

"Celeste Rebecca Levi, slow down." She froze midstride, and he noticed Lorrie Ann's eyes go wide. He must have managed to use his best angry-dad voice. Somewhere in the past couple hours, he'd switched to autopilot. He felt empty. He eased Rachel to one side of the large L-shaped sofa and moved a cushion under her leg.

"Sorry, Daddy. I wanted to show Miss Lorrie Ann my room." With a hand on the railing, she took one slow step down. Dub went to the stairs and picked her up, swinging her above his head.

"Higher, Grandpa, higher!" Her laughter filled the cabin.

"Dub, you're not helping." John went to the kitchen to retrieve a bag of frozen peas.

"Humph." He pulled his granddaughter close and tickled her before he looked up at Lorrie Ann. "Hello, I'm Dub Childress." Celeste wrapped herself around his barrel chest and pushed his gray felt hat back, kissing his cheek.

"Grandpa, this is Miss Lorrie Ann. She's my new friend. She let me cut my own grapes."

"Maggie and Billy's girl? I remember you. Weren't you a few grades behind Carol?"

"Yes, sir. Carol Childress? Oh, she... I'm sorry."

John watched as awareness then pity filled her gray eyes. He knew what would come next. On cue, she became awkward as she looked around the room, moving to the double glass doors.

"This is not what I expected when I heard they had added cabins to the farm. It's beautiful and comfortable." She ran her fingers along the rock edge of the fireplace, stopping in front of the family picture he had on the mantel. She quickly turned.

"I thought they were summer rentals. I didn't know they had them rented for living."

"Maggie was nice enough to take us in when we had nowhere to go." John adjusted the frozen bag on Rachel's leg. "Dub gave us the old homestead to live in, but it needed to be gutted and made livable, so we are here until I can get that finished."

Lorrie Ann hurried past him. "Oh, Maggie said to make sure you ate dinner."

In the kitchen, she started making beeping noises with the microwave.

He'd grown accustomed to women trying to feed him, but it was a first for one to take over his kitchen.

"You don't need to heat that up for me."

"Have you eaten?"

"No."

"Well, then, you're getting a warm meal. I promised Aunt Maggie."

Dub chuckled and John shot him a glare. Dub's bushy gray brows shot up but he remained silent.

Celeste's head jerked and her eyes popped open.

"Thank you for taking care of Celeste." John watched his baby girl fight sleep and smiled.

Dub stood. "She can be a handful. That's for sure." With those words, he laid Celeste in the wingback chair. "Well, I just wanted to see the little bits and make sure they were okay." He moved to the entryway and paused. "If you need anything, John, call me. I'm heading to Houston tomorrow, but I can cancel."

"Dub, go on to Houston. We're fine." He pushed Rachel's hair back from her face.

"Nice seeing you again, Mr. Childress." Lorrie Ann had moved to the sink and started running water.

"Please call me Dub. And welcome back. I know your aunt must sure be happy."

"Lorrie Ann, you're not washing the dishes." John tried to make his voice sound firm.

"Um…yes, I am."

Dub chuckled again and headed out the door.

"Really, Lorrie Ann, you don't have to do the dishes."

The microwave went off, and she turned to get the food out. Setting the plate on the counter, she dug around for some silverware.

"The girls are asleep. Come eat or Aunt Maggie will get mad at both of us."

He sat and attempted to give her a smile, but it felt more like a halfhearted contortion.

"Anything else I can do for you tonight?" She looked around the small kitchen.

"No, we're good, and you can report back that I ate." He saluted her with his fork before taking a bite.

After a few more mouthfuls, he set the fork down and made sure he had solid eye contact with Lorrie Ann before saying anything else. "Again, I want to thank you for keeping Celeste. She can be a bit high-strung, and some people find her energy level overwhelming."

"I deal with musicians and agents on a daily basis. Handling high energy and mood swings is my specialty."

Her sweet smile was at odds with the image he had of a music-industry insider from California. As she walked out of the cabin, John followed her. "You must be exhausted driving in from California today. Have you spoken to your mother yet?"

She stopped at the steps with her hand on the railing, turning back to him. "My mother? How do you know Sonia? I haven't heard from her in over three years."

"Oh." He didn't know what to say. Sonia had wanted to be sure of her sobriety before talking to Lorrie Ann. She should have contacted her by now. If she hadn't, he had just opened a nasty can of night crawlers. "She visits Maggie."

Lorrie Ann's eyes went wide. "Really? Do you know where she's living?"

"Have you asked Maggie?" He needed to talk to Maggie and find out what was going on. He had promised Sonia to keep their talks private. Did that include her daughter? He knew she struggled with guilt over her past with Lorrie Ann, and guilt did weird things to people, led to bad decisions. Was she still avoiding Lorrie Ann?

"I'll do that." She paused for a minute, her lips tight. Glancing down, she broke eye contact.

John waited, and when she brought her gaze back to his, she smiled and whispered, "Good night, Pastor Levi."

"Please, call me John."

He watched as she made her way back to the ranch house. An unfamiliar loss at her departure settled softly in his chest.

He wanted to spend more time with her, hear her laughter and watch her smile. He shook his head and turned back to the cabin.

It had been thirteen years since he had asked someone out on a date, and he had ended up married to her.

He stopped. Where had that thought come from? Unwanted memories surfaced, and John closed and locked the door, both physically and mentally. Even contemplating a relationship with Lorrie Ann needed to stop.

He felt confident in his work for God and tried hard to be a good father, but he had made a lousy husband. He wished he could close the door on the hurt in Carol's eyes as he locked the door behind Lorrie Ann.

His wife had deserved a better husband, but by the time he'd realized that, it had been too late.

Chapter Five

Tuesday slipped by quietly into Wednesday morning. The sun slid through Lorrie Ann's window, and she just lay there. A slow smile eased across her face when she realized she had nowhere to be, no appointment to make and no people to mollify or manipulate. She could lie in bed all day if she wanted.

Her forehead creased. She did have one thing she needed to do. Quick thumbs and the text to Melissa, the lead singer of the band, was sent. With a satisfying thump, she closed the drawer with the cell phone inside. She had a few weeks to hide.

Shoving the guilt aside, Lorrie Ann reminded herself that everyone deserved a holiday, and hers would be in the Lone Star State this year.

She sighed. What she really needed was a new job. There was no way she and Brent could work together. If her boss, Melissa, had to pick between the talented but troubled drummer and the band's manager, Lorrie Ann figured she would be the one to go.

Once dressed, she headed outside. Bible in hand, her other hand trailed over the smooth worn cedar railing of the zigzag stairs leading to the river below the cabins. The cool October breeze ruffled her hair as she made her way to the edge of the Frio. The flow of the river had changed since she'd left.

With her hand on one of the large cypress trees, she slipped off her shoes and stepped into cold, clear water. In California, she'd been so focused on being successful she'd misplaced her love for the outdoors.

"Miss Lorrie Ann, Miss Lorrie Ann. Hello!" Celeste's excited voice drifted down from the top of the cliff.

Lorrie Ann cupped her hand over her eyes to block the sun as she turned to find the six-year-old hanging over the edge of their balcony. "Hi to you, Celeste. Hear you're coming over today for a visit."

"Daddy has to take Rachel in to get casted. Can we cut some more grapes?"

"Sure. Thought we could make some cookies, too."

The little girl started to jump up and down. "Yeah! We can take some to Amy." Celeste leaned over the railing, suspended over the cliff.

"Celeste Rebecca Levi, put your feet on the floor right now!" John's stern voice came from the cabin door behind Celeste.

She looked back to the cabin and pointed down to the river. "Sorry, Daddy. Miss Lorrie Ann's in the river."

A few seconds later he appeared next to his daughter, one arm wrapped around the precocious six-year-old. "Hey there, Lorrie Ann. Hope you're well rested." His mussed hair fell across his forehead as he looked down at her. "Isn't the river cold?" The sun emphasized the highlights streaked in his dark blond hair. She knew men who paid hundreds of dollars to get coloring like his. Without a doubt, nature created his color.

"Maybe, but it feels good." She shrugged and smiled up at them, placing her hand over her heart. "I believe I should be reciting from *Romeo and Juliet*."

His laughter soothed her as much as the clear water running over the rocks.

Nose wrinkled, Celeste leaned over and asked, "What's Romeo and Julie?"

"Juliet," John corrected.

Lorrie Ann threw her arms wide. "A love story with a tragic ending. Poor Romeo stood under Juliet's balcony and professed his undying love."

"Then Daddy should be Romeo and you, the beautiful princess. Is Juliet a princess?"

"Monkey, I think Lorrie Ann wanted quiet time, not a literary discussion." He picked her up and swung her onto his hip.

"Quiet time? But that's boring." One small arm wrapped around her father's neck, Celeste slanted over the edge with a puzzled look on her face. "Miss Lorrie Ann, were you really wanting quiet time?"

"Well, I was thinking about finding a place to pray and think."

"Oh, I'm sorry. Daddy likes quiet time, too. But he does it at the church. Maybe you can go to the church with Daddy."

Even from the river, she could see the lines around John's eyes deepen with his smile. "Come on, monkey. Let's leave her to her solitude." He patted her back. "Sorry about the interruption, Lorrie Ann."

"Oh, please, don't apologize. I'll see you in a little bit, rug rat."

"Bye, Miss Lorrie Ann. Tell God hi for me." She waved as John turned them toward the door. "Daddy, what does *literinary* mean?"

Lorrie Ann couldn't stop the smile as she looked down at her toes beneath the water. Curious little minnows started checking out her feet.

In a few hours, the family would be eating dinner together before heading to Prayer Night at the church. The smile slipped away. Thinking of her cousin, Yolanda, caused old hurts to boil up from the deep places she thought buried.

Back then she had been afraid Aunt Maggie would side with her real daughter. Lorrie Ann remembered living for the day she would leave this small town, proving to everyone she mattered. Truth be told, she was still a little afraid what would happen if Aunt Maggie had to choose between them.

With a deep breath she closed her eyes, focusing on the sounds around her: the water, the wind dancing through the trees and the leaves floating to the ground.

"God, I've come back to find You. I know it's been a long time, and I'm not sure what to do. I've messed up so much I need You to show me the way to go." She stepped farther into the river. "I don't want Aunt Maggie to be hurt. Please show me what to say to my cousin, Yolanda."

She waded down the riverbank to a little platform. On the other side a ladder dropped down to a swimming hole with a long flat rock creating a natural edge. Above it hung a thick corded rope.

Climbing to the platform, she sat and dangled her legs in the water. Running her fingers along the pages, she opened her Bible to the prayer in Ephesians and read how much God loved her.

A noise on the steps alerted her to someone's presence. Turning, she raised her eyebrows at the sight of Celeste hopping down the stairs with one hand on the railing.

When the little girl spotted Lorrie Ann looking at her, she crouched on the step and whispered, "Are you finished with your quiet time?"

Lorrie Ann closed the Bible and grinned. Who knew a child could be so entertaining? "Yes, rug rat. Does your father know you're down here?" She glanced up to the cabins.

"He sent me over to Aunt Maggie's house." She skipped the rest of the way to Lorrie Ann and sat down, crisscrossing her legs. With her elbows on her knees, she rested her chin on her intertwined fingers. "Are we still talking to God or the fish?" She intently stared into the water.

"Um…well, I kind of ran out of things to say to God, and I've never talked to fish before. You talk to fish?"

Celeste rolled her legs around and flopped onto her tummy. With one hand under her chin, she dipped the other in the water.

"Yes." She looked up at Lorrie Ann with a big smile. "It tickles when they nibble on you. They're my pets." She moved her gaze back to the water. "Shh…there's Rainbow—he's the biggest." They both sat still staring at the fish underwater as he stared back at them. They waited in silence. Lorrie Ann smiled when she realized she was in a staring contest with a fish.

"Celeste Rebecca Levi!" They both jumped at the sound of John's voice. "I told you to go to Aunt Maggie's house. You are not allowed down by the river." His long strides had him by their side in seconds. "You can't be interrupting Lorrie Ann's prayer time."

He stood over them, hands on his hips. Lorrie Ann arched her neck back to look up at him. It just seemed wrong that a man of God would look so good. Wasn't there some rule about pastors being old grandfatherly types?

His cotton polo shirt fit just right over his broad shoulders and tucked neatly into his jeans. In silence, he stared down at them. Celeste jumped to her feet, her small body mirroring her father's stance as she fisted both hands on her hips.

Lorrie Ann squirmed, feeling like a kid caught skipping school. "Oh, it's all right. I saw her and called her down. I…um…finished—" she waved her hand in circles "—you know…praying."

He raised one eyebrow and grinned at her, probably amused about her stumbling over words he used all the time.

"Daddy, Rainbow almost came to me. You scared him away." She looked back into the river, searching the clear deep water for the fish.

He crouched down, balancing on his heels. He rested one hand on Celeste's shoulder and brought his gaze to rest on Lorrie Ann's face. "Are you sure she's not bothering you?"

For a minute she couldn't breathe, feeling lost in his eyes, but she managed to shake her head.

"Well, then I'm heading out. Are y'all good for the day? Need anything before I leave?"

Lorrie Ann gave a quick nod, still unable to speak.

"Give me a hug, monkey." He held his arms open.

Celeste leaped at him, kissing his cheek. "Love you, Daddy. Hurry back."

"We'll be back for dinner. See you then, Lorrie Ann." He flashed another heart-stopping smile and then headed up the stairs. Her gaze stayed locked on him as he bounded up the steps, two at a time.

"Do you like Daddy?" Celeste had flopped back on her belly, hanging her chin over the edge of the platform.

Lorrie Ann shot a startled frown at the back of the little girl's head. "What do you mean?"

Celeste twisted back around and wrinkled her nose. "A lot of ladies at the church look funny at Daddy, the way you just did." She threw a small rock into the water. "Some of them said I need a mom." She threw another rock. "Rachel says they're just busybodies wanting to marry Daddy and we don't like them." Jumping to her feet, she started gathering some more small rocks. "You're fun. If you wanted to be my mommy I wouldn't be mad. Rachel might be, though."

The bottom of her stomach fell. The thought of being anyone's mother horrified her.

Celeste started tossing the rocks sideways. "Rachel knows how to skip rocks. Daddy told me to keep practicing and I'd get it." She wrapped her fingers around another rock, her tongue sticking out between her teeth.

Lorrie Ann held her breath as she watched the rock fly. With a slight skip, it bounced back up once before dropping under the water. A huge smile filled her face.

Screaming, Celeste turned to Lorrie Ann, jumping up and down. "I did it! I did it! Did you see?"

Lorrie Ann laughed and clapped her hands. "Yeah! That was awesome, Celeste!"

As she twirled in circles, the little girl's ponytail swung out. "I skipped a rock!"

Out of breath, Maggie appeared at the top of the stairs. "Lorrie Ann? Celeste? Is everyone all right? What happened?"

Lorrie Ann laughed aloud, her smile feeling too large for her face. "Celeste skipped a rock!"

"I did! I did, Aunt Maggie! It skipped right over the water just like Rachel's and Daddy's." She squeezed her hands together in front of her, her body trembling.

"Celeste, you scared me half to death. If you two are going to make cookies for tonight, you had better get up here. No more lollygagging." With those words, she turned and disappeared.

"What do you say? Ready to go up and make those cookies?" Lorrie Ann dusted off a bit of gravel and leaves from her black cropped pants.

"Please don't tell Daddy. I want to surprise him."

"No problem, rug rat. Um…and you won't mention anything about the funny way I looked at him, right? I don't want him or Rachel to worry." She didn't know whether to laugh or cry at the thought of her, married to a small-town pastor.

Celeste pulled her out of the altered universe when she grabbed her hand, looking at her as if she'd gone crazy. She snorted. *Crazy* was a good word for her life.

"It's okay, Miss Lorrie Ann. Daddy says gossiping about people is hurtful. I won't tell your secret."

With that, the rug rat skipped up the stairs.

Great—the only thing between her and complete humiliation was a precocious six-year-old.

Chapter Six

As Lorrie Ann approached the kitchen later that evening, she faltered a moment and took a deep breath, willing the knot in her stomach to ease. With her best let's-do-lunch smile, she tossed her hair back and stepped through the archway, one high-heeled boot at a time.

She had spent thirty minutes changing into and out of clothes. In the end, she'd put on her Los Angeles armor.

Reaching out with both hands, she greeted her cousin. "Yolanda! It's been so long."

Yolanda's dark green eyes widened and for a second her mouth dropped open as her gaze took in the burgundy leggings and the silk blouse. But then again, Lorrie Ann thought, her cousin's surprise might have something to do with the five-inch brown leather boots that covered her knees.

Yolanda pushed the loose ends of her hair from her face, trying to adjust her ponytail.

Yolanda had taken after her dad in height and stood about seven inches taller than Lorrie Ann. Because of the boots, they almost met eye to eye.

"Oh, wow, L.A., you look—" Yolanda stepped forward into a quick hug "—great. It's been so long."

Maggie joined them. "Now, Lorrie Ann, I told you this

was a casual family dinner." Her gentle voice had an unusual sharp edge. "Why did you get all dressed up?"

"This?" Lorrie Ann ran her hand over her silk shirt. "It's my first family dinner in twelve years." She gave Yolanda a tight smile.

Yolanda bit her lip. "Excuse me. I need to clean up." With a glare to Lorrie Ann, she brushed past her and headed down the hallway to her old room.

Turning back to the kitchen, Lorrie Ann met Aunt Maggie's dark eyes. The smirk fell from her face, and she felt as if she had been caught stealing Uncle Billy's last cookie.

"What?" With her arms crossed, Lorrie Ann suppressed the need to squirm under her aunt's scrutiny. "I didn't do anything." She gave a heavy sigh and rolled her eyes. *Okay, so I have officially reverted to an insecure teenage girl.* "People expect me to be a certain way, you know, coming from Los Angeles and all."

"*Mija,* if you give people a chance, they will like the real you."

Lorrie Ann turned away from the gentle look in Aunt Maggie's eyes. Why did guilt feel so heavy and ugly?

She moved to the stove. "I'll finish warming the tortillas." As she flipped the tortillas, she heard a vehicle pull into the driveway. Celeste came rushing into the kitchen from outside.

The screen door slammed back as the hurricane of energy swirled into the room. "Lorrie Ann! Aunt Maggie! Rachel has her cast! It's purple."

"Hey, rug rat. Slow down."

"Rachel's so slow because she has to walk on the crutches and won't let Daddy help her. Aunt Maggie, Uncle Billy said to bring him the veggies."

Maggie grabbed the bowl and headed to the grill, ordering Lorrie Ann to make the tea while rubbing Celeste's head. A few breaths later, a knock on the door announced the arrival of John and Rachel.

"Hello?" John walked through the screen door then stood with his back holding it open and flashed a grin. "She insists on walking without my help."

The sound of Rachel's shuffling feet and the thump of the crutches came with agonizing slowness as they waited for her to make an appearance. When she finally made it to the door, John reached out to help her over the threshold.

"I have it, Daddy." With an awkward movement, she adjusted the crutch and managed to step up as her tongue stuck out in concentration.

John turned his face to Lorrie Ann, rolled his eyes and shook his head. "She can be a bit stubborn." He shot her a wink. "Gets it from her mom."

Celeste scooted a red step stool by the sink and started pulling out plates from overhead. "I'm stubborn, too, just like Mom. Grandpa says so."

"Celeste, get down from there! Wait until I can help you." One of John's hands stayed on the door as he tried to reach for his younger daughter with the other.

Lorrie Ann moved to Celeste. "Here, let me help you."

"Rachel always sets the table, but now I get to do it." The stack of thick milk-glass plates wobbled over her head.

Lorrie Ann reached up behind her to balance the plates and lower them to the counter.

Rachel twisted toward her father. "She can't do my job."

"Rachel, she just wants to help." His large hand covered her entire shoulder. "With the crutches, how would you carry the plates?"

"How about setting the silverware?" Lorrie Ann pointed to the table. "The basket's already there."

"Thanks," John whispered close to her ear as he walked past her to help Celeste carry plates and glasses. "I see you're back to your L.A. gear and artificial height?"

Standing in the kitchen with John, her decision to change

made her feel shallow. She gave him the same weak line. "I wanted to wear something special for my first family dinner."

With his arms braced behind him, John leaned against the sink and watched the girls set the long table. "You looked nice this morning."

She shrugged and flipped another tortilla.

"Oh, you look so pretty, Miss Yolanda," Rachel suddenly called out.

Lorrie Ann turned and saw the perfect example of feminine refinement walk into the kitchen. Her cousin wore a soft green dress with a faint floral print. It swirled around her knees and complemented the low-heeled sandals on her feet. Her thick brown hair now floated in waves just below her shoulders. Lorrie Ann straightened her spine and repeated her mantra, *Smile, stand tall, fake it if you have to.*

"Daddy, I want to dress up!" Celeste jumped up and down, clapping her hands. "Can I have some pirate boots like Miss Lorrie Ann?"

He laughed as he caught the six-year-old up in his arms. "I'm not sure a ranch is the best place for pirate boots."

Yolanda opened the cabinet door next to John. "L.A. did always love costumes."

Lorrie Ann felt like growling as she watched her cousin bat those incredibly long lashes at John. Instead, she repeated her mantra a few more times.

Yolanda continued in her soft Texas drawl, "Good evening, Pastor John. How did the trip to the doctor go today?"

"All went well. It was a clean break."

Celeste slipped out of his arms and ran off to get the napkins. Turning back to Lorrie Ann, he reached for the sugar as she poured boiling water over the tea bags.

He held out the container for her. "I want to thank you again for keeping Celeste. She went on and on about the plans you had today."

Taking the sugar from him, Lorrie Ann smiled. "To tell

you the truth, I looked forward to it myself." She looked up and was struck by the gentleness in his light brown eyes. For a moment she studied the gold flakes that radiated warmth. Oh, what had she been saying? "Um…she's a great kid."

"Please, let me know if she becomes too much."

Yolanda came up and laid her hand on his sleeve. "You know I can watch the girls whenever you need help."

Before he could reply, Aunt Maggie and Uncle Billy brought in the fajitas and grilled vegetables.

"Is the table set? Ice in the glasses?" Maggie set the platter of meat and bell peppers on the table and smiled. "Looks nice, girls."

"I got the plates and glasses, Aunt Maggie." Celeste ran from the table to the refrigerator. "I can get the ice, too!"

In a voice too prim for a young girl, Rachel yelled after her sister. "Celeste Rebecca Levi, you need to sit down." She lowered her voice and squinted. "You're going to give Daddy a headache."

John's rich laughter filled the room as he lightly pulled Rachel close to his side. "Thank you, sweetheart, but I think I'll survive."

Uncle Billy got the ice instead. After bringing out the rest of the food, Aunt Maggie sat down next to her husband. "Come on, everyone. Let's eat before it gets cold."

Lorrie Ann reached for her old chair and collided with John's hand. They both yanked back.

"That's Daddy's chair," Rachel informed her. "He always sits there next to me."

"Oh, I'm so sorry."

"No, you take it." His now-familiar grin made her forget about dinner. "We don't have assigned seating—just creatures of habit." He looked over at Rachel. "It's good to shake up our routine."

Uncle Billy's gruff voice snapped the air. "Can y'all sit down so I can pray?"

"Yes, sir," they answered at the same time. She slid a glance to her right and found Rachel glaring at her. To the left, John had his head bowed. Everyone joined hands. The words of her uncle's prayer slid into her heart. She had missed being part of this family worship.

As soon as the prayer finished, Aunt Maggie jumped right in. "So, Pastor John, have you had any ideas about the Christmas pageant? With Martha out of town, I don't know how we're going to get it all done. It is the hundredth anniversary, so it needs to be big."

Dread slipped through Lorrie Ann. She carefully put her filled tortilla back on her plate. "Aunt Maggie, please don't."

"Oh, *mija,* it's perfect." She handed a warm tortilla to her husband, never taking her gaze off John. "What about Lorrie Ann?"

She had to stop her aunt before she went any further. "No way."

John raised an eyebrow. "I don't think she's interested, Maggie." Filling his tortilla with meat and avocado, he shrugged his shoulders. "Vickie said she'd do it."

Yolanda snorted "Vickie? She's an awesome seamstress, but organizing and directing? She doesn't know the first thing about music."

Lorrie Ann thought of any suggestions she could make. "What about Mrs. Callaway, the high-school drama teacher? I remember her directing the pageant when I sang."

"That *is* Martha." Yolanda made it sound as if she should have known Mrs. Callaway's first name. "Her sister's having health problems, so she went to Houston to stay with her."

Aunt Maggie pointed her knife at Lorrie Ann. "Someone with the experience of organizing big music events is sitting right at this table."

Lorrie Ann gripped the knife, beating down the frustration. Disappointing her aunt seemed to be her forte. "No one in this town would want me anywhere near the pageant."

"Oh, pish-posh, that is just nonsense. The committee has been praying for someone to step up and lead the pageant." She looked at John as she poured Yolanda more iced tea. "Don't you think God is at work here?"

He took the opportunity to fill his mouth with his fajita. She watched his throat as it moved with each swallow.

The poor man needed to be rescued. "Aunt Maggie, I organized rock concerts not…church plays," Lorrie Ann tried to explain one more time.

"I can do it," Yolanda offered. "I've helped with the set and props for the last few years."

"You've done a great job, *mija,* but we need someone with a big vision. It is the pageant's hundredth-year anniversary."

Yolanda's salad became an innocent victim, each stab fiercer than the last. Her eyes stayed focused on her plate.

"Lorrie Ann played Mary when she was eleven. Remember?" Aunt Maggie looked back at John. "She's gifted with a voice so sweet." Her hands waved upward. "Her singing brought everyone to tears. You know she went to Los Angeles to start a singing career."

John smiled at her, eyebrows raised. "So that's how you got into the music industry."

Under his gaze heat slipped up her neck. "During college I discovered Hollywood was full of good singers waiting tables." She shrugged. "On the other hand, people who could organize musicians, not as common."

Yolanda pushed her beans around, talking to her plate. "I played Mary the following year." Another stab. "But Martha didn't let me sing."

"Oh, *mija,* you were born with your daddy's voice." Maggie patted Yolanda on the arm before looking back to John. "You might have noticed in church, he couldn't carry a note if I stitched a handle on it." She chuckled at her own joke.

Uncle Billy shook his head and took another bite of his fajita.

"Aunt Maggie!"

"I don't think she wants to—" John started.

"Daddy, I'm supposed to be Mary this year!" Rachel interrupted. "But with my leg I can't walk with Joseph."

John took a deep breath before answering. "Sweetheart, we'll find something for you to do."

Now Lorrie Ann wished she had let him sit next to his daughter.

Celeste bounced in her chair next to Yolanda. "Can I be Mary? Can I?"

"No! You can't—you're too young," Rachel bit at her sister. "Daddy, I've been waiting to be Mary all year!"

Lorrie Ann struggled with placing an arm around Rachel's shoulders. Maybe she should just talk to her. "There are other parts just as important to the story."

Lorrie Ann's heart broke at the sight of the girl fighting back tears.

The ponytail bounced with a nod. "I can be in the choir again." She leaned forward to see her father and blinked her eyes before forcing a smile on her face.

Lorrie Ann gave in and placed her hand on Rachel's arm. "What about a narrating angel? Talk to the shepherds and warn the wise men. We could use one of the farm's cherry pickers to lift you above the audience. Then you wouldn't even have to walk—you'd be flying." She gave Rachel a tentative smile. "You'd make a perfect angel."

Aunt Maggie flashed an I-told-you-so grin. "Look, she is a natural—already solving problems."

Lorrie Ann rolled her head back. "No, I just—"

Celeste sat on her knees and clapped her hands. "Please, Miss Lorrie Ann. I want to be in the play."

Rachel snapped at Celeste again. "You're too young."

Lorrie Ann softened at the sight of the small drooping shoulders. Her tiny kindred spirit pulled at her. Against her better judgment, she threw out another idea. "Maybe the kinder group can open the pageant with candles."

John's sharp intake of breath gave her the first clue that this might not be her best idea, the look on his face her second.

"Celeste with fire…real fire?"

The tiny shoulders popped up and the clapping started again. "I could do it." She practically stood in her chair. "Oh… Oh… What about Jenny, Mark and Carlos? We could all do it!" She threw her arms over her head. Yolanda encouraged her to sit back down and glared at Lorrie Ann.

"See, I can't do this."

Rachel looked at Lorrie Ann with steel in her eyes. "Kindergartners are too young to be in the pageant."

Lorrie Ann turned back to John. "Sorry."

His warm smile made her feel worse. "We'll work it out. God has a plan."

"What about you, Pastor John? You could lead the music part."

Rachel glared at her again. "Daddy doesn't do music anymore."

Uncle Billy tapped his watch, drawing all their attention.

Aunt Maggie jumped up from the table. "Oh, my, look at the time. We need to head over to the church for the prayer meeting. Pastor John, you're going to be late."

Lorrie Ann started gathering dishes.

"Oh, don't worry about those. Lorrie Ann, you go with Pastor John. Yolanda, we have to pick up Dolly." Without another word, she followed her husband out the door.

Chapter Seven

Lorrie Ann watched the screen door bounce shut with Aunt Maggie's quick exit. She sighed.

A heavy trepidation fell on her shoulders. The thought of going to the church and facing all the people from her past made her want to curl up under her quilt and never come out.

Her hands had a slight shake to them as she carried bowls to the counter and started covering them with foil.

She closed her eyes and drew in a slow deep breath. Feeling calmer, she turned back to the table and gathered more dishes. "I'm not going. I'll stay here with the girls and clean up." She focused on her voice sounding casual and nonchalant, throwing a smile over her shoulder for good measure.

John had started to scrape the dishes, and his light chuckle caused her to think she wasn't as successful as she imagined.

"Oh, no, you don't. After the Wednesday-night prayer meeting, the girls have choir. The committee meets while they're singing." He leaned a hip against the counter. "You can get information on the pageant. No commitment just information. I promise."

John took the glasses out of her hands and placed them in the sink.

"Someone once told me, we always do what Aunt Maggie says." He ended that sentence with a wink.

"Smart man." Unable to resist his charm, she smiled.

Celeste giggled while she held the door open for Rachel. "Lorrie Ann, you get to ride with us."

She needed a way out. "I can bring the girls home for you." She opened her eyes wide. "Don't you have some kind of vow to help damsels in distress? Come on. Please, give me an excuse to leave the committee meeting early. You would be rescuing me from the dragons roaming the streets of Clear Water."

His laughter rumbled deep from his chest.

"I think you're confusing me with a fairy-tale hero. Besides, the dragons aren't bad. Their intentions are good, even if a bit meddlesome at times." He looked her straight in the eyes. "Anyway, *helpless* is not a word I would associate with you."

A grateful smile eased across her face. "It's nice that you think that of me."

John cleared his throat and moved to the door. "We need to leave." She ran across his mind more than he would ever admit.

"Come on, Pastor John—taking the girls home will give me a good way out. Please?" She placed a hand on his sleeve.

He focused on her face. "Okay. You bring the girls home." He held the door open. "Come on, Lorrie Ann. Rachel's beating us to the truck. Can you manage in those boots or do you need help?"

With a flip of her hair, she rolled her eyes and passed him to walk through the door.

John tried not to be aware of the exotic-smelling perfume mixed with sunshine. It had danced through his dreams all night. He popped a green Jolly Rancher in his mouth and followed her to the truck.

Sliding behind the steering wheel, he noticed Lorrie Ann as she glanced over her left shoulder at the girls in the backseat. She then leaned toward him and whispered in a hushed voice, "I just want to warn you, taking me to the church is asking for a disaster in your chapel. Don't be surprised if lightning strikes."

He felt one eyebrow pop up as he bit back another laugh. Man, she was fun. Leaning in, he winked at her and whispered back, "God never actually struck anyone down with lightning, not in the Bible, anyway." That was so lame. He had to stop himself from groaning aloud.

It had been years since he'd flirted, but really, was that the best he could do? How had he ever managed to get Carol's attention?

He closed his eyes briefly. The images of his wife sitting on the floor and listening to him sing flashed in his mind. She had loved his music. Up until the point his music had become more important than her or God. Opening his eyes, he stared at the hand that used to wear his gold band. He had put those mistakes behind him along with any thought of starting another relationship.

With locked jaws he put his truck in gear and headed to the church. He needed to focus on his daughters and work.

Pulling into an empty parking spot on the main street, John slipped out the door with just a smile and wink. Lorrie Ann sat frozen as she watched him trot across the small manicured lawn in front of the town's picturesque church, complete with white clapboard, steeple and beautiful stained-glass windows. He greeted people at the large double doors that stood open.

If she had her way, she would have stayed in the truck. Instead, Celeste grabbed her hand and dragged her out of the safe cocoon of the cab. So with a deep breath, she reminded herself to smile, stand tall and fake it as long as she needed to.

Rachel, already out, swung her crutches and looked back with a scowl. "Hurry, we're late."

Lorrie Ann decided to ignore the curious and shocked faces as Celeste led her through the doors and to the front pew.

"This is where we sit," Celeste whispered. She turned and waved to a little boy a few pews over.

Rachel gritted her teeth and pulled her sister down. "We're already late, so behave."

Lorrie Ann closed her eyes. *Great—a few days in my company and the pastor shows up late to his own prayer meeting.*

Sitting up front worked out well because she could focus on God and ignore the peering eyes behind her.

The prayer meeting only lasted about thirty minutes. People took turns reading assigned scriptures. Requests and praises were shared, and finally John led the group in one last prayer.

As people started moving around, Lorrie Ann saw her aunt slide out the back door of the church.

Lorrie Ann looked down at the girls, not sure where to go. "What now?"

Rachel rolled her eyes and started pulling herself up. "We go to the children's building for choir. You need to head to the fellowship hall for the committee meeting."

Celeste grabbed her hand. "Come on. I'll show you."

John joined them as they passed the back doors. "Hey, thought you three beautiful gals could use an escort." He winked at Lorrie Ann.

"Daddy, you're so silly." Celeste giggled as he tickled her. They moved out the back door and walked across the small courtyard. Celeste held her father's hand then reached over and grabbed Lorrie Ann's fingers.

She relaxed when Katy Norton, now Buchanan, opened the door for them. It had been nice to reconnect with her friend from high school. Now Katy corralled a group of boys into the next room. "Rhody! Paul! Take these boys outside." She turned to Lorrie Ann with an all-encompassing hug. "I didn't get to greet you earlier. I'm so glad you came. Maggie came by the store and said you would be taking charge of the annual pageant."

John gave Katy a quick hug. "Well, we got her here, but no agreements yet."

Katy patted Lorrie Ann's arm. "Oh, it'll be good. I was so excited when Maggie told me you might do the pageant. I love the mysterious ways God works." She hugged her again. "I've got to go. Poor Abby has all eighteen girls by herself. I'll introduce you to my boys later."

Together she and John headed to the fellowship hall. Lorrie Ann's knees started to feel rubbery, and it had nothing to do with the stone walkway or her high heels. As they approached the back door, nausea rolled down to the pit of her stomach. She stopped.

Lorrie Ann could already feel the heavy judgmental stares like stones thrown at her soul. Why had she let them convince her going to church would be okay?

Whispers screamed her unworthiness. She didn't belong in this community. She could be a Christian without going to church.

"Lorrie Ann?" John's fingers gently braced her wrist, bringing her back to the present. The concern in his voice mirrored the worry in his eyes. "Are you okay?"

She turned from him to study the moths fluttering in the security light at the corner of the building. She could march in there with all the confidence she carried in L.A., but she didn't feel like pretending tonight. She'd made a huge mistake coming here.

Moving away from John, she shook her head. "I'm fine. I'm going to the car." She closed her eyes. No car...trapped. "I'll...help the girls. Katy...um...had a roomful of kids."

"She has Rhody, Abby and Paul to help with the children's choir." He grinned at her. "Man, you must really be scared if you'd rather spend the next hour with a bunch of kids than face the adults."

His words triggered a flash fire of outrage through her body. Her hands fisted at her hips. "Scared? I'll have you know there is nothing these people can say or do to me—"

Stepping back, he threw his hands up, palms out. "Just a little joke." He tilted his head and looked her straight in the eye. "A vein looks like it's about to derail from your neck." He gently put his hand on her shoulder. His smile faded and compassion filled his gaze. "Don't go in if it upsets you this much. But you could also focus on God instead of these doubts and fears."

He offered his strength, and she wished she could accept. She pulled back and wrapped her arms around her ribs. The blue door leading to the fellowship hall taunted her. "The last youth night I attended, Vickie told everyone I had parked under Hammond Bridge with Tommy Miller, the quarter-back. I knew they had gone to the prom together, but I always thought she and Jake Torres liked each other. I know Jake liked her. I thought Jake and I were friends, but…" She bit down hard on her tongue.

She glanced again at the moths dancing around the light. It looked welcoming and safe, but she knew how it burned if you got too close. "Then she started a rumor that I left with Jake. I can't believe he's a state trooper now."

She twisted her silver bracelets around her wrist. "Both those guys seemed to follow her around everywhere, so I never understood why she lied about me being with them. Jake and I were friends, but Tommy never even gave me the time of day until the rumors started. I should have ignored them, but everyone believed her." She couldn't bring herself to tell him what had hurt the most. She stood alone while Yolanda walked past her to join Vickie's group. They turned their backs to her, giggling and whispering.

The old pain felt just as fresh as it did then. She had become the outsider again. Unable to comfort the seventeen-year-old girl she had been, she closed her eyes.

John approached her, his fingers warm and strong as he squeezed her shoulder. She turned her head away, not wanting him to see the weakness of her stupid tears burning her lids.

She shrugged. "Without knowing why, I had been exiled from the group." Her eyes burned and her voice sounded harsh to her own ears.

How could something from twelve years ago hurt so much? This was why she never talked about the past.

"Lorrie Ann, fear will stop us from living the life God meant for us to live." He kept his gaze on her. "You don't have to go in with me, but I think you'll find it friendlier than your teenage memories."

The sincere concern in his golden-brown eyes jabbed at her self-pity.

She forced a smile. "Truthfully, I had some very unchristian experiences in that building." She tossed her hair and stretched her spine until she stood an inch taller. "But I'm a grown-up now and need to act like one." Maybe this was why God had brought her back. With a firm nod of her head, she placed her other hand over his.

John moved in front of her and waited until she made eye contact. "Lorrie Ann, people will hurt us. It's unfortunate but true. We all have our weaknesses and insecurities." He smiled. "God's always true. You have to trust in Him…with all things."

"I just don't want you to get caught in the cross fire. You're a very nice man."

He rolled his head back and groaned. "Oh, no." He fixed his stare back on her face.

She stared back with a blank expression. What was he talking about?

The corner of his mouth pulled to one side, giving her a lopsided grin.

From inside the fellowship hall, Aunt Maggie tapped on the kitchen window. Sliding it open, she called to them. "Lorrie Ann! Pastor John! What is taking you two so long? Come on in. Everyone is waiting."

Leaning in close, he looked her directly in the eyes. "Are you sure you're ready?" He held his arm out to her.

She smiled at John's gallant gesture. She had asked God for a sign, and now she walked back into a church on the arm of its pastor. Maybe now she should start trusting God. She had already waited twelve years. Nodding, she placed her hand on John's arm and walked through the blue door by his side.

Chapter Eight

Like dominoes falling, silence moved from person to person as each became aware of Lorrie Ann's entrance with John. Memories connected to the smell of lemon beeswax and coffee filled her head.

Aunt Maggie stood at the counter making fresh coffee, a broad smile on her face. "Lorrie Ann, come over here."

Avoiding eye contact with everyone, she headed straight to the safe harbor. Maybe if Aunt Maggie had been there twelve years ago it would have ended differently.

She had Lorrie Ann unwrap the homemade desserts and arrange them next to the coffee. People started milling around, pouring coffee and filling small plates with cookies, cake and pies. Many even greeted her, welcoming her back. Tension eased. Everyone had a smile for her.

Lorrie Ann made a quick glance around the small crowd, looking for Yolanda. She spotted her at a table on the far side of the room, next to Vickie. *Great!* Her warm-and-fuzzy feeling might have been a bit premature.

Vickie glared at Lorrie Ann with her arms crossed over her chest.

Please stay over there, please, please. Vickie moved toward her. Lorrie Ann's spine deflated for a moment.

With bold strides, Vickie headed straight to the dessert bar. Lorrie Ann fought back the somersaults that started low in her belly. Tossing her hair over her shoulder, she took a slow sip of her coffee, never taking her eyes off Vickie's sour face.

"What are you doing here?" The sugar-sweet tone of Vickie's voice didn't hide the malice puckering her mouth.

Lorrie Ann allowed the silence to linger. Her gaze traveled around the room until it landed back on Yolanda, still sitting at the far end of the room. Her cousin twisted a strand of dark hair around her fingers as she chewed on her bottom lip. The whole time Yolanda's crossed leg jerked up and down.

Vickie started squirming, stretching her neck. "So?"

Keeping a bored look on her face, Lorrie Ann shrugged and took a bite of a snicker-doodle Celeste and she had made earlier. "Aunt Maggie thought my expertise could help, and Pastor John offered me a ride." Taking another bite of the cookie and a sip of her heavily creamed coffee, she paused before asking her own question. "What are you doing here?"

Vickie leaned in and whispered, "I belong here."

John stood at the head of a group of tables pushed together and called for the meeting to start. After commanding everyone's attention, he called Lorrie Ann over to him.

She smiled at Vickie. "Excuse me. Pastor John needs me."

Her smile fell a bit when she noticed all eyes on her. Nevertheless, she moved to the front and sat down in the empty chair next to John. She squirmed a bit in the metal chair, feeling guilty for the pettiness of her last thought about Vickie. She really needed to grow up.

"First, I want to thank each of you for being here. The giving of your time and talents makes this annual event a special testimony to God's love." He turned to Lorrie Ann and smiled.

The bottom of her stomach fell out, but she made sure her own smile hid any discomfort and anxiety. *Fake it, girl.*

"Many of you know Lorrie Ann Ortega as Billy and Maggie's niece. She also happens to have experience managing and organizing large musical events. Fortunately for us, she's visiting for the holidays, and Maggie, Katy and I are working on her to lend a hand in the absence of Martha. She's come tonight to see what we have and what we need. So, please share any information you have that might convince her to assist us."

Applause filled the old fellowship hall. Lorrie Ann relaxed.

Maggie started handing out packets. The rest of the meeting ran smoothly, and, keeping an eye on the clock, Lorrie Ann jumped up to get the girls. Her goal: reach the back door without talking to anyone.

She stopped breathing as Jake Torres made his way toward her. Being a state trooper fit him. In high school, he had walked across campus with purpose and power. All the girls loved him, and she had counted him as a friend. When he'd remained silent in the face of the horrible rumors, it was clear who was more important to him. Vickie was part of his crowd, and they reminded her she would always be the outsider. Of course, Lorrie Ann had heard Vickie had ended up married to Tommy, so he had been on the losing end also.

She remained stiff as Jake pulled her into a quick bear hug. "Let me officially welcome you back."

Even with her heels on, she only reached his upper chest. In her silence he continued. They were all adults now; she really needed to get over the old hurts.

"I wanted to thank you. Not everyone can keep calm at an accident site. You helped the girls and John. I imagine it wasn't easy for him."

Lorrie Ann smiled and nodded as she waited for something ugly to enter the conversation. How could he talk to her as if he didn't know his silence had destroyed her life in Clear Water? It was twelve years ago; maybe he forgot.

He just smiled and kept talking as if they were long-lost friends. She knew if she wanted to grow in her faith, she'd have to let go of some of this bitterness. But really? Not even one small *sorry?*

"You should help out with the pageant. I'm the construction chair this year. There's about twelve of us on the committee, and basically we can build anything you throw at us."

John joined them. The men greeted each other before he turned his attention to her. "I have a financial-committee meeting, and it'll probably go late." He glanced back to Jake with a wary grin. "JoAnn and the ladies want to buy a new vacuum cleaner, and George and his boys think it's a waste of money."

Jake laughed, patting John on the back. "It's good seeing you, Lorrie Ann. I'm outta here before someone needs a peace officer."

She managed to nod. Once alone, John tilted his head slightly to the right. "Are you good?" He spoke softly.

"The church is still standing. I'd call it a victory." She grinned and tucked her hair behind her ear. "But I'm still not sure I want to take on the pageant."

"Maggie'll have all the information you'll need." He handed her the keys. "Ready to take the girls home?"

She smiled as relief flooded her body. "That's the plan. I'll go get them." She paused. "Thank you, John."

She slipped out of the door, heading to the children's building. Her steps were light, feeling as if she had conquered some childhood fear, but her celebration might have come a little too early.

Vickie ambushed her halfway down the curved sidewalk.

"Hey, don't walk away from me." Vickie grabbed Lorrie Ann's arm and spun her around.

Too tired to put up with the attitude, Lorrie Ann pulled her arm free and kept walking.

"The way you throw yourself at Pastor John is wrong," Vickie hissed at her back, following her. "You're pathetic in your cheap boots and L.A. ways. You stay away from those little girls. They need a real mother."

Lorrie Ann froze then slowly turned and faced her high-school nemesis. Silence filled the air between them, the minutes stretching out. Lorrie Ann prayed for the right words, to harness her anger. Her pulse raced as her breathing grew heavy.

The past twelve years disappeared. Inside, Lorrie Ann felt like the seventeen-year-old girl that never stood up for herself. She put her fisted hands on her hips and opened her mouth to give it all to her. "Vickie, you need to…" Lorrie Ann paused.

Anger and bitterness radiated off Vickie, her chest raising up and down in quick motion. Vickie stood alone. Lorrie Ann thought about her living in a trailer on her parents' property and working at the local grocery store, the one-time prom queen divorced by her perfect quarterback sweetheart, Tommy Miller.

Immediately Lorrie Ann pulled back her words. They came from her anger, not God. She turned her back and went to collect the girls.

Vickie, Jake and Tommy still seemed to have some left-over issues. She refused to be pulled into high-school drama again. She had her own problems to deal with in order to figure out her own future.

Lorrie Ann rested her hand on the light switch in John's bedroom. He'd thought with Rachel's hurt leg they should sleep downstairs, and he would sleep on the sofa. Growing up with her mom, Lorrie Ann's only bed had been the sofa in whatever apartment they'd stayed in. No adult had ever given up their bed for her.

She had tucked the sheets around his daughters, and now they looked so little in his big bed. "Good night, girls. Lights out. I'll be in the living room until your dad gets here. Okay?"

Celeste popped up. "No, we're not done!"

Lorrie Ann paused to think what she might have missed. Nothing came to mind. "Well, let's go over the list." She touched one finger. "Bath?"

"Check." Celeste bobbed her head.

Lorrie Ann smiled and added a second finger. "Pajamas on."

"Check."

"Teeth brushed."

"Check."

"Backpack ready for school?"

"Check."

"I can't think of anything else."

"You forgot something." Celeste giggled and sat with her legs folded under her.

"Um…a drink?"

"Nope."

"Uh…let's see." She racked her brain trying to figure out what she had missed. "A good-night kiss?"

"Nope." She bounced her legs. "Silly, Daddy does that."

"We got the pillow and blankets out for your dad." Lorrie Ann looked from Celeste to her older sister. "Rachel, can you give me some help here?" A slight shrug was the only response. The silent treatment had pretty much held up all night.

"Let me think." Pinching her nose, she closed her eyes and a new thought occurred. "Oh, I have it." She snapped her fingers. "Your prayers."

"You're closer." The six-year-old stretched out the two words. "We do those after the next thing."

Lorrie Ann drew her brows down in confusion. "After what, Celeste? Please just tell me."

Celeste crossed her arms over her small chest and pouted. "You have to guess."

"Celeste, your father told me you would drag out bedtime, so I can just turn off the lights and go to the living room."

With a heavy sigh, Rachel flopped to her back. "Celeste, give it up." She looked back to Lorrie Ann. "She wants a story. Daddy and Amy always read us a story before we turn out the lights. You don't have to." Twisting her back to them again, she pulled the covers over her head.

"Oh. Sorry, your dad didn't say anything about a story, and I'm kind of new to this bedtime-ritual thing." Lorrie Ann realized this was the sort of stuff she had missed growing up. What a surprise that these two girls could teach her so much.

Celeste looked confused. "Your mom didn't read you stories at bedtime when you were little?"

"Well, she was busy, so I just went to bed." She didn't think it was appropriate to tell them her mom was either passed out drunk or partying with her latest boyfriend.

She patted Celeste's leg under the quilt. "I would love to read you a story." Glancing around the room, she didn't see any children's books. "I could make up a story. I did that a lot growing up. I didn't have any books, so I would make up my own stories."

Celeste clapped and bounced in the bed.

Lorrie Ann laid her hands on Celeste's shoulder. "Careful of Rachel's leg."

"Oh, sorry. Can you make up a story about a princess?"

Lorrie Ann tapped her finger on her lips. "I do happen to know about one princess, but she didn't know she came from a royal family. A jealous duke wanted revenge on his brother, the king. So, he stole the king's most precious treasure. Do you know what he took?" Lorrie Ann noticed Rachel had turned back to them.

"His golden crown?" Celeste whispered.

"Good guess." Lorrie Ann smoothed Celeste's hair from her face. "But it wasn't gold or jewels. His newborn daughter slept in a basinet laced with colorful ribbons. The duke hired a villain to steal the infant and kill her. But when he went to strike her, he stopped. Her innocent face looked up at him, and his black heart melted. So, instead he took her to the woods where coyotes roamed and left her nestled in the roots of a giant oak tree."

Celeste wiggled under the covers and pulled her stuffed animal closer.

"Hearing the soft whimpers, the mother coyote came to investigate the strange noise in her forest. She curled her body around the babe, giving her warmth through the night. Close by, an isolated cabin stood. Rumors about the old lady who lived there swirled in town."

"Did she find the baby?" Celeste yawned.

"Maybe." Lorrie Ann stopped the story when Celeste's lids fluttered down. She ran her hand over the child's wayward curls.

"More story." The two words came out slurred as her eyes fluttered shut again.

"Next time, rug rat." She smoothed Celeste's hair away from her face. Looking across the big bed, she found Rachel watching her. "Night, Rachel."

"Good night, Miss Lorrie Ann." The soft reply gave Lorrie Ann a strange and unexpected sense of peace.

Stepping out into the living room, she checked the time. Eight forty-five. John said he'd be home before ten. She plugged her laptop in and opened her emails.

She touched base with Melissa, who told her Brent had gone into rehab and reassured her that after the holidays they would talk. It didn't matter how much Brent apologized or if he got sober, she was not going to have that drama in her life. Lorrie Ann refused to become her mother.

She sent and replied to a long list of emails then followed up with some texts. Glancing at the time, she finally shut her laptop down. It was almost ten.

Anticipation fluttered across her nerves. Lorrie Ann looked at the front door, imagining John walking through it. Standing, she moved to the glass doors at the back of the cabin.

Her mind drifted back to the conversation she and John had been having before going into the fellowship hall.

The room became too small. She stepped out onto the deck and left the door open so she could hear the girls.

John walked into his quiet house. Lorrie Ann's presence lingered in the air. The idea of her waiting for him to return home felt good. He immediately pushed that thought out. Carol, his wife, should be the one he wanted here. With her death he had made a conscious decision to stay out of any romantic relationship. Lorrie Ann was someone new and just making him aware of his loneliness. The girls needed all of his focus; he would remain strong in this choice to remain single.

After checking on the girls, he made his way to the back of the living room toward the sliding glass door. He noticed a pillow and extra blankets folded neatly on the sofa. He had told Lorrie Ann to put the girls in his room. He smiled. It was nice of her to set those out for him.

He stepped through the open door to the back deck. Somewhere a bonfire burned. The breeze carried the smoldering scent of mesquite and cedar through the air. At the edge of the deck, Lorrie Ann stood with her fingers wrapped around the worn-smooth wood railing.

"Lorrie Ann?" He spoke softly, not wanting to disturb the mood of the night.

Lorrie Ann sighed, her fingers relaxed. She kept her eyes closed.

He walked across the deck but made sure to keep his distance from her. "How did the girls do? Celeste give you any problems?"

"No, they were great, and I actually got a good bit of work done after they went to sleep."

She would not make eye contact with him. He studied her profile. He could see Sonia, her mother, in her bone structure. Had she made some of the same mistakes as her mother while living in L.A.? Well, she was here now and seemed to be looking for answers. He would treat her like any member of his congregation in need of help.

"Good. Thank you for helping. I'm sure this has been a rough week for you." He moved to stand next to her. He turned to the side, his left hip resting against the railing as he crossed his arms.

After a few moments of silence he continued. "I know your aunt means well, but she can have the tenacity of a pit bull when she gets an idea in her head." He tucked his hands into his front pockets. "I don't want you to feel obligated to help. Guilt can be a strong motivation, but it's not the right one." Turning parallel to her, he braced both arms on the cedar railing. "Your aunt is so excited about you being home she might miss the point of you being here."

He loved Maggie's passion, but he also knew she could steamroller people into what she thought was the right thing for them whether they agreed or not.

His fear now was that she had decided to play matchmaker. He rubbed his eyes. That was all he needed. Forcing a smile on his face, he looked back to Lorrie Ann.

John gave Lorrie Ann a half grin that made her want to melt against him and tuck her head over his heartbeat. She had to wonder, how did the women of his congregation concentrate on his sermons? She shook her head and looked back at the landscape. Maybe it would be better if Yolanda had brought the girls home.

Silence stretched out between them. She struggled with her thoughts and what she wanted or what she should do. *Stick to the plan, girl. Get your life in order and head back to California.*

His calm voice pulled her out of the vicious cycle of her thoughts. "Just take your time and please don't let your aunt blackmail you into doing anything."

The tension eased a bit. She rolled her shoulders and twisted her neck, forcing her body to relax. "Thanks. It's not that I don't want to help. I just don't have anything to give right now." She could make out his nod in the dark.

With his encouragement, she continued, "I'm the last person anyone wants at the church." She rubbed the back of her neck and gave a halfhearted snort. "I'm way too flawed to be directing anyone about the birth of Christ."

"See now, there's where you're wrong. Sometimes it's the imperfections in our lives that make us the perfect choice to help others."

She snorted. "I have never been the type to help others. I'm pretty much a look-out-for-myself type of girl."

He grinned. "Yeah, I can see that."

Turning away, Lorrie Ann focused on the outline of the surrounding hills. After what seemed like an eternity of silence, she could not resist a glimpse back at John, but the moment she made eye contact, her muscles froze. He had set a trap, and like an experienced hunter, waited for her to enter. The warmth of his eyes held her in place as strongly as an iron cage. Heavy stillness sparked the air around them.

He took a step closer, his right hand wrapped around the smooth wood, a butterfly's touch from her fingers. She tried to swallow, but her mouth had gone sand dry.

"I…" She what? Shouldn't be here, had already fallen in love with his girls, needed to go back to L.A.…wanted to kiss him. She felt her skin tighten and heat up. "I…um." She needed the ground to open and pull her under, that's what she needed.

This gorgeous, perfect man standing in front of her had two little girls and he worked for God. A few steps and she would be safe on the other side of the door. Focused on the escape, she willed her feet to move.

His hand left the railing and gently touched her arm. "Lorrie Ann, it's okay. You don't have to volunteer for the Christmas pageant. But if you could help me with the girls while you're in town I would appreciate the time."

An invisible hand guided her gaze back to his face. That was her excuse, anyway.

"This might be hard to believe, but most people find Celeste just a bit overwhelming." He pushed his hair away from his forehead and stared at the surrounding hills. "Rachel can be so closed off and reserved. She has a hard time with new people in our lives. They both love Amy, but she's out for a couple weeks while she recovers." He turned back to her. "They seem comfortable with you."

Rachel...liked her? He had to be joking or blind. After a long pause, she decided he must be blind. "You know they see Amy as safe. They don't have to protect you from her."

"Safe? Protect me from what?"

She saw confusion on his face. Poor man. "The women in this town who want to either marry you or set you up with someone in their family."

"That's ridiculous." He jammed his hands in his front pockets.

"Rachel told Celeste to be careful when the ladies are nice to her because they want to date you." She smiled. "According to Rachel, you have to be protected from the ladies because you're busy doing God's work and saving people."

"Celeste told you this?" His words, slow and pronounced, came one at a time.

"Yes. They don't worry about Amy. You're too old for her, and she doesn't have any family members they have to worry about."

John turned from her and leaned his forearms on the top railing with his fingers entwined. One polished burgundy boot rested on the bottom. The mesmerizing eyes that had held her now contemplated the night sky.

She had tried to be funny, but her efforts seemed to have fallen flat.

"Every decision I made after Carol's death was for the girls' sake. How did I miss this?" His low voice sent an arrow straight to her heart.

"You're a great father. Some parents never give a thought to how their decisions affect their children. Don't beat yourself up over this."

Once again, his full attention fell on her face. His eyes moved over every inch, resting on her left check. "You told Maggie you got the bruise from the accident. But you had it earlier in the day."

She turned away from him. He didn't seem to care about what had happened twelve years ago, but how would he feel if he knew the truth of her choices in the past two years?

She flashed him a full smile. "That's my story and I'm sticking to it."

"Okay, we'll leave it at that for now. So what about the girls—will you help me out for the next few weeks?"

She shrugged. "Are you sure you want me?"

He gave her a simple nod.

"Okay, how can I be of service?"

"I take them to school in the morning, but I need someone to pick them up other than Monday. I get them on Monday. They get out of school at three-fifteen. I'm usually home by five, unless there is an emergency. Wednesday night I'd need you to bring them home like tonight. Get them tucked into bed. That's it."

"I think I can handle that. I really like them. You've done a great job."

"Thanks. I paid Amy…"

"Oh, I'm not taking your money. I'm just helping out. Use

the money for something more…I don't know…useful, like a vacuum cleaner."

With a low chuckle, he turned sideways, leaning on the railing, and smiled. "So you don't have use for money? Independently wealthy, are you?"

A flash fire surged through her body. "I'll have you know, I have worked hard for every penny. I…" She paused at the sight of his raised brow and smirking lips.

Taking a deep breath, Lorrie Ann calmed herself before continuing, "Sorry, I can get a bit defensive." She glanced at her watch. "Oh, I need to go. You have to get up early and I'm keeping you."

"Let me check on the girls, and I'll walk you home."

Following him into the cabin, she stopped at the bedroom door, allowing him to go in alone. She felt like an intruder as she watched him whisper something to Rachel. His daughter settled back into her pillow, and he kissed her forehead before moving to the other side. He straightened the sheets Celeste had kicked off, her small body sprawled across the king-size bed. The thought of the little girl not even remaining still in sleep melted her heart a bit, and it scared her.

In a few weeks she would be back in L.A., and attachments led to hurt. She was already regretting her agreement to help out. She needed to get better at saying no.

She moved away from the bedroom door to lean against the hallway wall. She pushed her tongue hard against her teeth and wrapped an arm around her stomach. She had to get out, away from John and his girls. Her hand grasped the handle.

"Lorrie Ann?" He moved beside her, his arm reaching across her to open the door.

For a second she imagined those arms embracing her. His voice brought her back to reality.

"Thanks again for helping. It's a huge worry off my shoulders."

John's presence warmed her insides with each step across the wooden planks of the deck. She longed to stay next to him, but those thoughts were dangerous.

Biting her lip, Lorrie Ann reminded herself of all the reasons she needed to remain distant from him. It was hard when just walking silently next to him comforted her. The spark of anticipation kept her wanting to know him more.

But she wasn't what he needed. Without a doubt, he would not like what he found. People didn't stay; it was best to be the first to go.

His voice yanked her from the spiral of depressing thoughts. "Um…Lorrie Ann, I was wondering what you were doing Saturday night. I have a friend from Houston who's an artist, and he's having an opening in Kerrville. It's his first solo show in Texas. I told him I'd be there. Would you join me? It won't be like anything in L.A., but he's an incredible artist."

She froze. Excitement, doubt and fear battled it out in her brain. She stared at him, unable to make a decision. Had he just asked her out on a real date?

The silence became awkward. His hand moved to the back of his neck and his eyes darted, glancing everywhere but at her. She had no idea what words to form. She felt her mouth open, but no sound came out. He finally broke the agonizing stillness.

"Listen, don't worry about it. It's just…I never invite anyone in town because it could lead to misunderstandings and assumptions. With you leaving soon, I just… It's no big deal."

"I'll think about it." Lorrie Ann's eyes went wide in surprise. *Don't overreact.* She shrugged and played with her bracelets. "I'll check to see if I'm busy." Lame. "Night, John." She turned away from him and walked as briskly as possible without actually running. Even though running did seem the best plan of action.

Chapter Nine

John hit the razor on the side of the sink and rotated his face around to check for any missed spots. He looked himself in the eye and berated the man in the mirror again. What possessed him to invite Lorrie Ann to Gary's art opening? He just got her to agree to watch the girls, so why did he feel the need to push himself into her life even more? After wiping the sink, John stepped out of the bathroom.

The startled look on Lorrie Ann's face when he'd asked had caused him to regret his impulse the minute the words left his mouth. Her hesitation and polite *maybe* didn't do much for a man's ego. He might have well said, "I'm asking you because I can't ask anyone else." *That was smooth.*

"Celeste, you're not helping!" Rachel's frustrated voice shrieked, derailing John's contemplation. With a sigh, John gave up all hope of a peaceful morning.

He shook his head and forced his thoughts back to the moment at hand and away from his new neighbor. Walking into the living room, he grabbed a green Jolly Rancher from a handmade ceramic bowl and popped it in his mouth. He needed coffee and real food, but this would do for now.

"Daddy, I can't wear the yellow socks with this skirt!" Rachel struggled to get off the sofa.

"I like it!" Celeste opened the refrigerator door.

"That's because you're six and don't care what people say about you."

The offended six-year-old stuck her tongue out.

John set Rachel's painkillers on the counter and turned to Celeste. "No breakfast until you're dressed and hair brushed. Go up and get another pair of socks for your sister."

Standing in a purple shirt with yellow polka dots two sizes too big and red mud boots, she looked down with a puzzled expression. "I am dressed, Daddy."

A dramatic sigh came from the living room. "See what I mean, Daddy? And you want her to pick out my socks!"

A knock on the door saved him from answering. Quickly turning to the entryway, he saw Lorrie Ann standing on the other side of the cut-glass door. He couldn't stop the grin from spreading across his face. Man, he felt like a twelve-year-old with his first crush.

"Mornin', Lorrie Ann." He stepped back so she could enter. "I wasn't expecting to see you until this afternoon."

"Good morning. I come bearing gifts from Aunt Maggie's kitchen." She lifted the plate up.

"Lorrie Ann! You brought…" Celeste sniffed the air. "Cinnamon rolls!"

"And coffee for your dad." She gave him a halfhearted smile. "Sorry about intruding, but Aunt Maggie worried it might be hard to get everyone ready this morning."

"Who would have thought one broken leg could knock a normal routine so out of whack." He sighed and looked back over his shoulder. "They're not finished dressing, and I still haven't made breakfast." He followed her to the kitchen. "Please, make yourself at home." As he slid past, the clean smell of her hair distracted him for a moment.

She looked up when he paused, and her brows rose.

He cleared his dry throat and lowered his voice. "Did you think about Saturday?" He jerked back when he realized he had his nose almost pressed into her hair. He looked down and found his youngest daughter in a wide-eyed stare. "Celeste, go upstairs and get the socks."

Lorrie Ann handed him the thermos and unwrapped the warm rolls. The rich smell filled the air, and his mouth watered. He adored fresh cinnamon rolls.

"I want the green ones." Rachel twisted around to face the adults.

John scowled. She wanted a green cinnamon roll?

"Daddy, please tell me you're not going to let her wear that outfit to school. I would be *soooo* mortified." She flopped her head against the back of the sofa.

John raised an eyebrow and paused in the process of pouring coffee into a mug. "Ah…you want the green socks." He closed his eyes and took a slow sip of the dark drink. "Why are you so upset over Celeste's clothes?"

She glared at Lorrie Ann. "It's her fault. She's trying to look like you."

"Me?"

"Rachel!" John's shocked voice over his daughter's rudeness joined Lorrie Ann's.

Celeste came to the railing. "I can't find the green ones!"

"They are in the closet in the basket on my dresser." Rachel hit her casted leg. "I hate having a broken leg."

"Rachel, you owe Miss Lorrie Ann an apology, and I don't see the problem with the yellow ones." John placed a roll on a small plate and carried it over to her, sitting on the edge of the ottoman. "What about white? They go with everything." He sighed as he watched her roll her eyes. When did she become a drama queen, and how did the color of her socks become so important?

He noticed Lorrie Ann moving to the stairs and raised his brow in a silent question.

With a flick of her hand, she pointed to the loft. "I'm going to retrieve the green socks and see what I can do to help Celeste's outfit choice. You and Rachel eat your breakfast—Aunt Maggie's orders." Her voice pitched higher on the last three words as she reached the top.

Rachel picked at her icing.

"You know you shouldn't let other people make you feel ashamed of your sister, and a broken leg is no excuse for being rude."

"I'm sorry." Glancing up from her plate, she looked into his face. "She doesn't get it, Daddy. They watch us, and if we do anything wrong they say it's because we need a mother."

Lorrie Ann's words from last night flew back to him.

He patted her knee. "Sweetheart, I love you." He paused, asking God for the right words. "You know people talk—that's just part of human nature. For the most part, they just want to help, and unfortunately, everyone has an opinion on what that looks like. You can't let them change you or your sister." He smiled at her. "That's my job."

"But you have a big job already, and Celeste doesn't make it easier."

Pounding on the steps brought his attention up.

"We found your green socks! And Miss Lorrie Ann pulled my outfit together!" She jumped down the stairs.

"Well, what do you think, Rachel?" Celeste twirled in front of them. The necklace Lorrie Ann wore this morning now worked as a loose belt with the large silver loops wrapped twice around the small waist, making the shirt look like a dress. A black turtleneck and tights actually looked good, and John grinned at the zebra-striped boots. He remembered the argument he'd had with his father-in-law over buying the pricey boots for a six-year-old.

Lorrie Ann pulled Celeste's newly done braid to the front. "We even found yellow ribbons to match."

"She could braid your hair, too. I brought green ribbons for you to match your socks." Celeste held out the sock and ribbons to her older sister.

"No, thank you. I like doing the ponytails Daddy taught me to do. I fix Celeste's hair and mine each morning." She took the sock and started struggling to get it to her foot.

"Rachel?" John sighed. Had she always been this defensive?

After a few heartbeats, Rachel responded, "I'm sorry for earlier, Miss Lorrie Ann."

He stood and kissed Celeste on the forehead. "You look great." Meeting Lorrie Ann's gaze, he smiled at her, surprised by the rightness of having her here. "Thank you, Lorrie Ann." He touched Rachel's shoulder. "Sweetheart, why don't you let Lorrie Ann braid your hair, so I can feed our monkey, okay? Then we will be off, and Miss Lorrie Ann can report back to the admiral that her mission was completed."

His oldest daughter nodded. She gave him a tentative smile as she pulled herself forward. Lorrie Ann moved behind Rachel and started weaving her hair.

His heart tightened. The older Rachel got, the more she looked like her mom.

What had he been thinking when he'd asked Lorrie Ann on a date? One look in his daughters' eyes should remind him that his selfishness had cost them their mother. In the past five years he had created a balanced life for his girls. Why would he risk that for any woman, especially one who would be leaving in a few weeks? He snorted at the thought as he poured milk for Celeste.

"What is it, Daddy?"

"Oh, it seems your dad forgot he's not nineteen anymore. Got things to do, places to go and girls to raise." He winked at her and tugged her hair.

"You must be getting old if you forgot all that."

The laughter burst from his gut. The other two females looked at him in surprise. He just smiled back.

John whistled as he stepped through the side door of the church leading to the offices in the back. Lorrie Ann kept invading his thoughts when he needed to focus on the message for Sunday.

"Pastor Levi, welcome back! Hope our girl is on the mend. We've been praying for her." JoAnn, the secretary he'd inherited four years ago, greeted him from her large oak desk.

He smiled and thanked her. No matter what time he arrived, she was always waiting for him with coffee and a schedule for the day.

"Here are your messages. With you being out, they got a little backed up. Mostly calls about Rachel and sending you prayers." She handed him a neat stack of white note cards. He knew each one would be precise and detailed. "Here is a list of activities. I rescheduled the meeting with the other pastors. Raymond Hill is back in the Uvalde hospital, so you might want to visit him. You and the girls have been invited to the Campbells' and the Lawsons' for Sunday dinner. I told the Lawsons you were already eating at the Campbells'. I knew you would want to spend some time with Amy."

He nodded, knowing better than to interrupt her morning drill. He played with the Jolly Rancher in his pocket and wondered what she would do if he popped it in his mouth. She had several rules for him, and life was easier when he followed them.

"We do need to talk about the Relay For Life fundraisers when you get a chance. The building committee has given you three dates for the picnic at the pecan farm. Let me know which one works for you, and I'll work with Maggie to get that set."

He tuned out, and his brain shifted to something more interesting—Lorrie Ann. He should treat Saturday like a date, including dinner. Oh, man, he hadn't thought of taking her to dinner. He didn't even know what she liked. He squinted and flexed his jaw. She liked Mexican food, so Mamasita's would be a good choice.

JoAnn startled him from his thoughts, her glare telling

him she was fully aware he had not been listening to her. Her four-eleven frame now stood firm in the doorway with hands on her hips.

"Sorry, JoAnn." He flashed an innocent smile, or tried to, anyway. By the look on her face, she wasn't buying the act. "What were you saying?"

She shook her head in disappointment then looked completely to the left and slowly to the right. Even though they were alone, she lowered her voice and became even smaller. John had to step in to hear her.

"Rhody and Katy Buchanan are in your office."

He gave the closed door to his office a puzzled frown and whispered back, "I didn't see any of their vehicles."

"They're needin' some marriage advice, but they don't want anyone to know."

Closing his eyes, he sighed deeply. The one thing he'd tried to avoid the past four years was marriage counseling.

JoAnn moved back to her desk. "Here are the business cards you always give out." Handing him three cards, she marched to the coffee and filled his favorite mug. "Such a shame. Young people just don't know how lucky they are to have someone to love, and those four boys…" She shook her head.

"They came for help, JoAnn, not a divorce. That's a good sign."

Pointing her finger to his chest, she looked him sternly in the eyes. "Yes, and a testimony to their trust in you."

Sometimes she acted more like a mother than an employee.

"Are you going to help them or send them away like you always do?" She thrust her sharp chin to the cards he had tucked into his shirt pocket.

With a crooked grin and soft sigh, he took the warm cup from her hands. "I *am* helping them, by sending them to a trained professional." If they knew the truth, he would be the last person they'd seek out for marriage advice.

"I'll pray for them." She moved to her desk. "And you."

"Thank you, JoAnn." He turned to the door and paused with his hand on the knob. He closed his eyes for a quick prayer, asking for the right words to give the couple he considered good friends.

Rhody stood and held out his hand in greeting when he entered. "Pastor Levi." Stiff voice, not the usual easygoing one John enjoyed.

"Sit, sit. Hi, Katy." He smiled and noted the framed photo she held.

"Oh, sorry. I was just telling Rhody what a great family picture. We've never been to the beach. You should've had someone else take it so you could be in the photo, too."

He nodded and watched her place the picture of Carol and the girls back on his desk, bracing for what always came next.

"It looks like Celeste is about one. This must have been right before the accident." The deep sadness glistened in the moisture of her eyes.

He nodded again as he took his seat, hoping to put her at ease. "It happened two weeks later. I keep it on my desk to remind me how fast life can change and the blessings we take for granted. Both the girls talk about that weekend at the beach as if they remember. They've watched the video a million times."

"That's nice." She swallowed and reached for her husband's hand beside her.

John took a deep breath and pulled out the cards in his chest pocket. "So what brings you in this morning?"

Alone, John sat at his desk, the earmarked Bible lying open under his hands. His thoughts turned to Lorrie Ann again. He glanced at his sermon. It needed a bit more polishing, but he couldn't focus.

Rachel seemed to be more on edge lately, or maybe it had

just been brought to his attention. He needed to add a daughter-father lunch date to his schedule.

In the process of reaching for his detailed itinerary, the framed photo Katy had moved earlier caught his attention. The only framed photo he kept on his desk always created conversation.

The soft sunset surrounded Carol's golden hair as she held a chubby Celeste on her hip. At her feet, Rachel smiled up at the camera as she tried to catch waves in her bucket. It showed the perfect family on a summer beach vacation. Katy had made the same comment many others had while smiling at the beautiful picture. "John, you should have had someone else take the picture so you could be with them instead of hiding behind the camera." He would chuckle, letting them assume he agreed.

He never corrected anyone, but he hadn't been the lucky one to take the picture.

When they'd been invited to go with some friends to the coast, he'd once again declined. He needed to finish a song and had meetings to attend. With his music career about to launch, he couldn't afford to take off. Upset, Carol insisted on taking the girls without him.

He traced a finger along the edge of her face. She'd begged him to go, but he'd believed at the time his music career needed him more.

After Carol's death, Julie, the photographer and friend, brought him the pictures and video. A reminder of the beautiful gift he'd taken for granted.

Lunch with Rachel sounded like a great idea right now. He went to call JoAnn, but before he picked up the phone, it rang.

"Mornin', John." The familiar voice came boldly over the line.

"Hey, Chuck," John greeted his mentor from the past fifteen years. "Good to hear from you. What's up?"

"Not much. Just going over my prayer list and realized we haven't spoken in a few weeks."

John chuckled. "So you're checking up on me?"

"Figured someone has to. No telling what goes on in that small town of yours."

"You'd be surprised. How're Jill and the girls?"

"Everyone's good. We found out that Karen and Eric are making us grandparents. One minute you're holding a baby girl in your arms, then you wake up one morning and she's having her own." Chuck sighed. "Speaking of daughters, how are your little ones?"

"Actually, right now we're dealing with a broken leg." John went on to tell him about the accident. He even admitted to the concerns he had in getting everything done, along with the fundraiser for the youth building.

"I didn't realize how much I needed to talk, Chuck. God's timing is as faithful as always."

"Call me anytime. In a small town, you have a bigger threat of feeling isolated. Tell me, how's the music coming along?"

John spun his chair until he faced the window behind him. "I haven't found the time between my ministry, the girls, remodeling the house and all the community events."

"It's a talent you've been given. I remember you always sitting at the piano or with a guitar in your hand. You were never without music. I know it helped through your parents' deaths."

John couldn't help but snort. "Yeah, look where it got me with my family. A wife I didn't get to spend enough time with and two little girls who didn't know me."

"John, stop punishing yourself. It's all about balance and sharing that gift with your girls. Do either of the girls show any musical talent?"

John smiled. "Rachel loves singing. She has a very mature voice for her age. Celeste will try any instrument she can get her hands on." He grinned. "Not that she can actually play any of them." He frowned and pulled in his lips. In his vow to keep music from his life, had he also deprived the girls? He rubbed his hand over his jaw and looked up to the clear sky outside.

"John? You there?"

He thought about the guitars and violins he had boxed up and locked away. "Yeah. I get a bit overwhelmed at times."

"Hey, that's why you need someone to talk to." His friend chuckled. "Even Jesus gathered twelve friends around Him. No one expects you to go it alone. We all need help."

John picked up a pencil and started tapping it off his knee. Leaning his head back, he smiled at the ceiling. "Now you sound like some of the women around here. They all seem to think I need a wife. My girls, on the other hand, have gotten it into their heads they need to save me from the women."

"Do the girls have someone safe to talk to?"

John froze in his chair. "What do you mean? They have me."

"Yes, but they also want to protect you."

"Now you sound like Lorrie Ann."

John closed his eyes, not able to take back the words. He could see the graying eyebrows arch in question. Like all the times he sat across from him.

"Lorrie Ann? Not to make this a big deal, John, but this is the first time I've heard a woman's name other than JoAnn's or Maggie's."

"Then don't make it a big deal. She's Maggie's niece from California and is visiting for a couple weeks. With Amy's injuries, Lorrie Ann is helping out since she's right next door."

"How old is she?"

"Really, Chuck? You're going to go there?"

"Hey, just because you're a father and pastor doesn't mean you can't have a social life. When was the last time you went out for fun with adults?"

"I don't need to have fun." John heard Chuck grunt. "Well, that didn't sound right."

"You didn't answer my question. When was the last time you went on a date?"

Silence.

"John, don't tell me in over five years you have not gone out once."

"I live in a small town, and when I say *small* I'm talking population four hundred and six, and that includes the horses. I don't know. It'd be more complicated than it's worth, and until now I've had no desire to go out. I didn't set out *not* to date. I just haven't met anyone worth the risk."

"Until now, huh? So, is she worth the risk?"

He spun the chair back around to face the sweet faces of his wife and girls. "Maybe."

"So, have you asked Lorrie Ann out?"

Silence, longer and heavier this time.

"Oh, boy, you have, and you don't know what to do next!" Chuck went into full laughter.

"I'm glad you're finding this amusing, mentor of mine."

Chuck coughed. "Sorry. Listen, I know it's hard to balance a personal life between church and family. Being a single dad makes it even harder, but really, you need to relax. Do I need to remind you God's in charge of all the days of your life? You have always been a bit of a control freak. Besides, the only way you'll find out if she's worth it is by spending some time with her."

"That's why you're my mentor, Chuck." He let out a heavy sigh and noticed the time ticking away by the minute on his clock. "I've got to be going, but this call could not have come at a better time. Thanks, Chuck."

"God is good, John. How about we close in prayer?"

John closed his eyes and focused on the words in Chuck's prayer, and he asked for his own heart to be open to God's will.

* * *

Lorrie Ann watched the SUVs line up behind her in the school driveway as she leaned against the BMW's silver hood, her brown leather boots crossed at the ankles. A few people waved at her, some stared, trying to figure out who she was, and others just glared. She smiled at them all, enjoying the irony of her, Wild Child L.A., in the soccer-mom line.

Worried about being late, she had been the first to arrive. She now stood where Aunt Maggie used to wait for her and Yolanda. Not much had changed. Everyone from preschool to high school attended the same campus, with the gym in the center of the buildings.

A few minutes after the bell rang, doors burst open and kids ran everywhere. Lorrie Ann thought about Rachel moving with this rambunctious crowd. Maybe she should have signed her out earlier.

"Miss Lorrie Ann! Miss Lorrie Ann!" Celeste ran across the playground with her backpack dragging behind her, stirring up the dirt. A small group of little people followed, and much to her horror, they all stopped in front of the BMW.

"See, I told you she had pirate boots! And she plays in a rock band, and she's going to let us be in the Christmas pageant." Celeste aimed her big smile straight at Lorrie Ann.

"I manage a rock band—I don't play in one—and—"

"Are you a real pirate?"

"She can't be a pirate, stupid—she's a girl."

"Girls can be pirates."

"Hold on, guys. Girls can be pirates if—"

"The car's top goes down into the trunk."

A chorus of aahs followed Celeste's announcement.

"Did you steal this car?"

"No!" How did one control a conversation with six-year-olds? They managed to make musicians look docile. She gave them her best stern look. "Celeste, would you please introduce me to your friends?"

"Oh, I'm sorry. This is Bethany, Daviana, Carlos, Colt, Jenny and Rey."

She sat on her heels to greet the short creatures eye to eye. "Nice to meet you. To answer your questions, I am not a pirate—I just like tall boots. Even though girls can be pirates, it's wrong to steal. I manage a band. I don't play in it."

"But you're going to direct the play and let us be in it, right?" Celeste wrapped her arms around Lorrie Ann's shoulders.

"Maybe." She shrugged. "I haven't decided yet." Another decision she had avoided since coming to town. The list kept getting longer.

"Please, please!" The chorus of high-pitched voices surrounded her.

"You look like you could use some help." Katy approached from behind her car. "Colt, are you causing problems?"

"No, Momma. We're helpin' Celeste to get Miss Lorrie Ann to run the Christmas play so we can be in it."

"Yeah, we want a rock star to help the play so it'll rock!" The kids laughed at Carlos's air-guitar jam and started jumping and cheering.

Katy laughed. "I think you have your own fan club. So, you're helping Pastor John with the girls?"

"Just for a week or so."

"You might as well agree to help with the play, too. I personally think it's a God thing. I know your aunt would be over the moon with glee." Katy winked at Lorrie Ann. "The people in this town could use a shot of something new. Pastor John, well, that poor man just needs a social life. You would be good for him."

Lorrie Ann stood and frowned at Katy. Why did everyone think they knew what that man needed?

"Come on, Colt. We need to find your brothers." Katy grabbed her son's arm. "Bye, L.A. I'm sure I'll see you soon."

The short people still stared at her. "Um…don't you have

people waiting for you?" As the little ones started running off, she turned to Celeste. "Where would Rachel be? Do you think she needs help?" She searched the buildings and playground. No Rachel. Great—first day on the job and she'd already lost one of the girls.

"She's probably just talking with her boyfriend and doesn't want our help. Are you going to date Daddy?" She took Lorrie Ann by the hand and started leading her to the small courtyard outside the fourth- and fifth-grade buildings. Lorrie Ann didn't really hear any of the girl's words after "boyfriend." Oh, that didn't sound good.

"Why do some people call you L.A.?" Celeste asked as she led her to the tennis courts.

"It's my initials for *Lorrie Ann,* and all I talked about in high school was going to California and becoming a big star. So people started calling me L.A. I liked it at the time."

"Do you like it now?"

"Not as much. It just doesn't feel like me anymore."

Celeste broke free and started running to her sister. "Rachel! We've been looking for you."

"I'm right where Amy always picks me up." Her glare darted from Celeste to Lorrie Ann. She was going to make a textbook teenager at this rate.

She motioned to the boy next to her. "This is Seth Miller."

"So you're the new babysitter," the boy snarled, flipping the long hair out of his eyes. He slumped next to Rachel, holding her hand, his hoodie and jeans looking two sizes too big for his slender frame.

Rachel hit him in the arm. "I don't need a babysitter."

"I'm not a baby either! And you're not supposed to be holding a boy's hand." Celeste crossed her arms over her chest, glaring at Seth.

"Maybe you should move to the other side of the table, young man." Lorrie Ann grimaced. Did she just use the term *young man?* "You're Vickie's son, right?"

He shrugged his skinny shoulders, dropping Rachel's hand and moving over. "I hear you drive a real sick car."

Lorrie Ann looked back the way they had walked. "Would it be easier if I just drove around to the tennis courts? You need to elevate your leg, Rachel."

Celeste scooted next to Seth, looking in his notebook. "What you writing?"

"Celeste, you come with me." Much to her surprise, she caught a grateful smile from Rachel. She felt way in over her head when it came to dealing with children and wondered what crazy bug had gotten in her brain that had made her agree to take care of these two.

"Seth is Rachel's boyfriend."

"Uh…does your dad know about them?"

"Nope." And with that one loaded word, Celeste skipped ahead.

Chapter Ten

A shirt landed on Lorrie Ann's head, blinding her for a moment. Raising her face to the loft, she caught the next piece of flying clothing before it hit her. "Hey!"

Rachel laughed as she sat with her leg high on pillows. "That's Celeste's idea of gathering up the laundry." She turned her face to the loft. "Don't forget my purple shirt with the black threading. I want to wear it for Spirit Day."

Lorrie Ann opened the closet with the stacked washer and dryer and started the water. "What about your dad's clothes?"

Rachel shrugged but kept her face in the book she read. The sky opened up and a downpour of girls' clothes flooded the living space.

"When was the last time you did your laundry?" Lorrie Ann asked as she picked up the small shirts, jeans and socks mixed with towels and sheets. "We're not going to get all this in one load."

She looked up to see Celeste swing from the top of the stairs.

"Celeste Rebecca Levi, walk down those stairs!" Rachel yelled before Lorrie Ann could say anything.

"I'm going to Jenny's pj party this weekend. We're going to sing and practice for the play." Celeste brought a basket over by the washing machine and started putting the sheets and towels in a pile.

"You can't go this weekend," Rachel said. "I'm going to Kendal's bowling party. It's a sleepover."

"Why can't you both go to your parties?" Lorrie Ann closed the lid and faced Rachel, puzzled over the girl's concern.

"I don't want to leave Daddy alone for a whole weekend."

"Oh, that's sweet, but I'm sure your dad can handle it. He's a grown man, and sometimes adults like to have their own time."

"Not Daddy. He told me he loves having us home with him and it's too quiet when we are both gone. Anyways, some of the ladies in town might use it as an excuse to bother him."

She thought of his invitation for Saturday. Maybe it wasn't a date so much as him wanting company. But why her?

"Well, he did ask me to go to Kerrville with him."

"You?" Rachel's voice sounded alarmed. Lorrie Ann decided not to take offense. Rachel cared about her father and wanted the best for him. She agreed. A wild child from L.A. was not it.

"We're just friends, Rachel. I'll be heading back to California soon." She put water in the kettle to make tea. "It sounds like you both have great plans for the weekend. Your dad would feel bad if you canceled because of him."

Celeste took her hand and led her to the other side of the L-shaped couch. "I told everyone you put my outfit together and did my hair. They liked it." She jumped and clapped her hands together. "I have a great idea. We can have a sleepover here, with you. You can do our hair and help us dress up. It would be fun."

"Daddy won't allow it. You know that."

"But if Miss Lorrie Ann stays then it's okay." She looked back to Lorrie Ann. "Daddy doesn't think it's smart to have our friends overnight because we don't have a mom. But if you stayed it would be okay."

"No, we have a mom. She's just not here," Rachel snapped. "She can't spend the night. It would cause even more gossip. You're such a baby."

Celeste planted her fists on her small hips and stomped a zebra-striped boot. "Am not."

It never occurred to Lorrie Ann all the land mines a single father had to step around, and being the local pastor just made it worse.

"I'm sorry, Celeste. I don't think it would be a good idea. Most of the moms don't really know me either."

Celeste crossed her arms. "You could still help with the pageant."

"You know what? I think I will. It's not as if I have anything better to do while I'm here. Sitting around will drive me crazy."

Clapping, Celeste jumped up and down. "Yay!" With a shout, she threw herself at Lorrie Ann and wrapped her small arms around her neck.

"But *she* will drive you crazy." Rachel shook her head and grinned at her little sister.

Turning back to sit down, Celeste stuck her tongue out. "I will not."

Lorrie Ann sat in the corner with a throw pillow under one arm. Celeste quickly crawled next to her as if it was the most natural thing in the world to curl up in Lorrie Ann's lap.

"Will you tell us more of your story?"

"My story?" Her forehead wrinkled between her eyes. She couldn't imagine Pastor John being happy with her telling them stories from her past.

"Yeah, the one about the lost baby princess." Celeste nestled deeper into Lorrie Ann. "The mother wolf protected her in the forest."

"Oh, that one. Well, let's see. We were deep in the forest,

right? Far away from the village, an old lady lived by a river. The people in town whispered about her weird behavior, evidence of her craziness." Lorrie Ann ran her hand through Celeste's silky strands. Glancing over at Rachel, she smiled. The girl's book lay open, but Rachel had her head back, gazing into the heavy rafters.

"Is she a scary old lady?" Celeste whispered.

"Oh, no, but because she was different, people stayed away. She wore every piece of jewelry she had collected over the years. The gold and silver rattled every time she moved."

"She didn't have a sister or husband?" Celeste asked.

"No, she lived alone. When she found the baby lying in the tangled roots of her favorite tree, she thanked God for the precious gift of a child she thought to never have. The old lady loved the baby but feared someone would hurt her, so they stayed deep in the woods. The secret princess grew strong. Her only playmates were wild animals of the forest."

"Didn't she want to play with other kids?" Rachel asked without ever looking at Lorrie Ann.

"Yes, she did, and as she got older she would ask about the world beyond their little cabin. She loved the woman she called Grandmamma, but in her heart she knew there was more."

Celeste turned so she could look up at her. "What about her daddy? Was he looking for her?"

"Celeste, if you would stop asking questions Lorrie Ann could finish the story."

The younger sister stuck out her tongue at Rachel. "You asked a question, too."

Lorrie Ann couldn't hold back the laughter. "You girls fight over the silliest things." A high-pitched whistle filled the cabin. "Come on, Celeste. You can help me make tea."

Celeste jumped up. "But what about her daddy—was he sad?"

"Of course. Every day people would come from far and

wide to report sightings of his daughter. Many even brought in little girls, claiming they had found the lost princess. However, he knew a secret that would prove to him his precious jewel had been found. With each proving false, his heart would grow a little tighter. But every year on the day of her birth he sent out five hundred doves, each with a message to her."

Celeste opened the refrigerator door, and Lorrie Ann put the iced tea in to keep cold. She added the garlic bread to the oven and took off the foil lid to the lasagna.

When they finished, Celeste pulled her back to the sofa. "Did a dove ever find her?"

"A few found their way to the forest, but the old lady chased them off. By now, almost twenty years had passed and the girl no longer wanted to wait to discover the world. Late one night she packed a bag and climbed out her window."

"Wait—if she was twenty, why did she have to sneak away?" This time Rachel turned to her and frowned. "She's old enough to live on her own."

"But the old lady wouldn't let her leave, right?" Celeste rubbed her hands together. "She was afraid of being alone."

"That's part of it. She also knew someone wanted to hurt the princess. She wanted to protect her from the dangers of the world."

The door opened, and all three turned their heads.

"Daddy!" both girls said at once.

Celeste ran to her father. The little girl's unguarded joy gave Lorrie Ann images of what she had missed as a young child.

John swung his more energetic greeter to his hip and kissed her on the cheek as she tangled her arms around his neck. "Hey, monkey. Mmm…the kitchen smells good."

"I helped Miss Lorrie Ann make dinner."

He slid his daughter to the floor. "You didn't need to start supper."

His gaze focused on Lorrie Ann. She made herself stop chewing on her upper lip and smiled. "You have enough casseroles in your refrigerator and freezer to feed a family for three months. We just threw one in the oven with the garlic bread. You want some tea?" She moved to get the pitcher, avoiding his probing eyes.

He chuckled and moved into the living room to check on Rachel. "A blessing or a curse of being a single dad in a small town? Every female in the area has a desire to feed us."

"Poor you. Well, I'll be going home. Rachel did her homework, and Celeste started a load in the washer."

John gave his daughter a quizzical stare. "You did a load of laundry?"

"Yes, I did! Miss Lorrie Ann helped me. But I separated the towels and whites like Rachel told me."

"Good job." With a smile that created a long dimple on his left cheek, he turned his attention to Lorrie Ann. "Why don't you eat with us." He hung up his jacket in the closet and pulled his tie loose. "I'm sorry. I told you I'd be home by five and it's almost five-thirty. You're probably ready to get outta here."

"Stay, Lorrie Ann!" Celeste grabbed her hand and started jumping up and down. "Tonight's game night. We can have four!"

"Stop embarrassing yourself, Celeste," Rachel scolded from the living area.

"Settle down. Lorrie Ann might have other business to take care of." John mouthed a *sorry* to her.

"No, no. It's okay. The smell of warm garlic butter has my mouth watering." Maybe it wasn't the food as much as the man.

"Good. We always seem to be the guest. We never get to serve from our table." He headed to the kitchen. "If I ever get our house on the ranch finished, we'll get to invite everyone to our home. I'll make the salad."

"Um…" All of a sudden, she felt as if she was playing house with Pastor John Levi, but instead of the dolls Yolanda used to have, this was with real children.

A family of her own had always seemed out of her grasp. She'd tried to force it with Brent, but look where that had gotten her.

Did God want her to see what she had given up? Lorrie Ann looked around for something to do so she wouldn't feel awkward. "I can chop something."

"Too late—all done." He held up an empty bag of precut salad mix. "What does it say about a society when we are too busy to cut some carrots and lettuce?"

The timer went off, and Rachel started making her way to the kitchen table.

Once seated, they joined hands and prayed. The feel of John's strong hand wrapped around her smaller one, while Celeste held her other, gave her a lump in her throat. She repeated each word of the family prayer and stored them in her heart.

After the prayer, easy chatter about their day filled the room. Lorrie Ann remained silent. She didn't want to destroy the warm, cozy ambience at the family table. For a moment in time, she was the mom of this beautiful family. Then guilt snaked its way up to her stomach. She wasn't their mom, and she had no right pretending even for a minute. This was the dream she never even knew lay buried in her heart, the dream she'd sacrificed at the altar of fame and success.

John laughed at something the girls said then turned his attention to her.

"What do you think, Lorrie Ann?"

"I, um…wasn't listening. Sorry."

"That's okay. So, how did the first day of pickup duty go?" he asked with a friendly smile as he took another bite of lasagna.

Oh, with everything else she had forgotten, she needed

to talk to him about Rachel's boyfriend. She had wanted to speak to him privately so as not to embarrass Rachel. She looked at both girls. They suddenly concentrated on their food.

"This isn't good. Who's going to tell me what happened? Celeste, did you cause problems?"

"It wasn't me. It was Rachel. She has a boyfriend!"

A frown creased his forehead. "Rachel? That can't be true."

The preteen had her hands under the table, her face focused on her plate.

John moved his glare to Lorrie Ann.

With a sigh, Lorrie Ann answered the question in John's eyes. "It wasn't that big a deal. After the playground cleared we couldn't find her. She was waiting on the other side of the school, sitting at the picnic tables."

Rachel picked her head up and looked at her dad. "That's where Amy always picks me up. Every day after school. Then we get Celeste off the playground. Celeste gets to play for a while, and the traffic clears out. It's what we did. I forgot to go to the car lineup today." She turned to Lorrie Ann and gave her a glare that rated off the charts. "That's all."

Celeste popped up on her knees. "No, that's not all. She was sitting with Seth Miller."

John tilted his head and raised his eyebrow.

"He's her boyfriend." In a singsong voice, Celeste chimed loudly. "K-I-S-S-I-N-G."

The shock on John's face would have been comical if not for the tension in the cabin.

"They were holding hands." Celeste made kissy faces at her big sister, unaware of their father's mood change.

"You're a baby!" Rachel yelled, leaning forward.

"Well, you were!" Arms crossed over her chest, Celeste flopped back in her chair.

"You're eleven years old." John's strong voice silenced the room.

"I'm almost twelve," she whispered after a period of quietness.

He looked at Lorrie Ann as if he somehow wanted to blame her.

"You know the rules about boyfriends." He covered his plate with the dinner napkin.

"We aren't dating, Daddy. We were just…holding hands." She buried her chin into her chest, which muffled her last words.

"How long has this been going on?" His jaw flexed.

"He asked her Wednesday night." Celeste provided the answer.

"At church? You're grounded." His sharp reply came fast.

"Why?" Tears hung in her eyes now. "I haven't done anything wrong. We…we…just held hands. He asked me to the homecoming dance."

"You're not going." John stood, taking his empty plate to the sink.

"Daddy, you already said I could go!"

"With your friends, not Seth."

"He *is* my friend."

Lorrie Ann felt like crying. Everything had been so perfect until she'd ruined the night. "I'm sorry." She started gathering the leftovers. "They were just sitting on the bench writing in a notebook."

"We were doing our English homework," Rachel mumbled. "May I go—" she looked up to the loft then around the cabin "—to your room? Please." She wiped her eyes with the back of her hand.

"Yes." John sighed and reached his hand out to cup his daughter's face. "I love you, but you're too young to date. We'll talk about this later. From now on, you will go straight to Lorrie Ann's car."

"Yes, sir."

Lorrie Ann started running water in the sink. "I ruined the family dinner."

He carried the remaining dishes to the counter. "No, you didn't. That's what families do. We laugh, love, fight, work it out and start all over." John braced his arms on the tile edge next to her. "Actually, this might be the first time Rachel has broken any of my rules." John started drying the dishes as she washed.

The domestic job had her feeling warm inside.

He set the towel down and turned to her, one hip rested on the edge. "Man, she's almost a teenager. I don't think I'm ready for a teenage daughter. I don't know how I'm going to do this without Carol. If I had my way, I'd just lock the girls away. What do I know about teenagers? Carol was the only girl I ever dated. I didn't even have a sister."

"You'll be fine. I personally think dads are the key to raising a self-confident girl."

He leaned in closer, about to say something. Her gaze stayed on his eyes, waiting.

"Daddy, tonight's game night. Can Lorrie Ann play with us?"

They both pulled back.

"Oh, no. I think I've done enough damage for one night. I'm going to be heading home."

John's golden eyes pierced her. "Why don't you play with us. You can pick the game."

Lorrie Ann wanted to linger, but what frightened her most was the desire to stay forever. He needed a stable woman in his life, not a walking disaster.

"Good night, rug rat." She kissed Celeste on the cheek. "I'm sure Aunt Maggie will be sending me over with breakfast again."

"Good night."

"I'll walk you out." He opened the door and waited for her

to walk through. "Dinner was nice, thanks. I don't remember the last time I came home to dinner on the table."

"Up until the middle-school drama." She stopped on the front porch. As much as her brain screamed for her to run as fast as she could, something else wanted to hang on and never leave. "Sorry about the boyfriend thing." She bit her lip and debated if she had a right to make the next statement. "About the dance—you should still let her go. I'm sure they would love to have you as a chaperone. My aunt and uncle attended all our dances when I was in school."

"You're probably right. Lorrie Ann, it's not your fault. She's growing up, and I'm going to have to find a way to deal with it." He shuffled his feet, his hands fisted deep in his pockets as he looked over the driveway toward the pecan orchard. He cleared his throat. "About Saturday...?"

She smiled. He reminded her of a middle-school boy asking a girl for his first dance. "I would love to."

His face turned back to her. "Really?"

"Yeah. The girls said they had plans with their friends and you didn't like being alone."

"Oh." Something crossed his face she hadn't seen before, but it disappeared quickly, and he flashed her his heartwarming grin. "I'll be working on the house until about two or three. I'm trying to get the remodeling done before spring. We can head to Kerrville about five. That should give us time to eat dinner then head out to the art gallery."

"Sounds good." *Back away, girl. Put one foot in front of the other.* She moved to the steps.

He followed her down. His boots crunched the red gravel walkway. She could hear the wind whispering through the branches as insects chirped and sang. The urge to hold John's hand caused her fingers to clench. She kept a safe distance between them. More important, she needed to keep her heart at a safe distance. A bad feeling washed over her that she would spend most of the night wondering what it would be like to kiss a pastor. Well, not any pastor—just Pastor John Levi.

John lingered on the edge of the porch, even after hearing the screen door close behind Lorrie Ann. Sometimes life changed so fast he felt out of control, but he couldn't remember ever feeling so alone. Walking to the front railing, he scanned the rows of pecan trees that stretched into the darkness. The stars appeared anchored in the velvet night sky, but under his feet it felt as if his world was shifting.

He didn't like this edgy, restless feeling that had been hounding him. Was it an awareness of Lorrie Ann as a woman or the idea that Rachel inched closer to growing up each day?

Both thoughts made him uncomfortable. It didn't matter how nice it felt having Lorrie Ann at the dinner table. He couldn't let his heart go there.

His head dropped between his shoulders. How could he raise two girls without Carol's insight and wisdom? Just the thought of Rachel dating… No, he couldn't let his mind wander down that path. Despite his love for Carol, he had neglected and hurt her. If he couldn't prevent that from happening, how could he allow himself to trust some kid with his daughter's heart?

"Daddy?" Celeste had her head poking out the door. "Can we play a game? Rachel is already asleep."

What he could do right now was hold his little girl and let her know he loved her.

"Come on, monkey. How about a story instead of a game tonight?" He led her into the living room.

"Sure!" She headed up the stairs and returned with a large hardcover book. With one arm wrapped around the children's story Bible, Celeste jumped onto the sofa next to him.

One thing he knew with certainty—there was no promise of a second chance. He pushed a few loose strands of hair from her face and kissed her forehead. "Which story do you want tonight?"

"The one about Joseph and Mary with baby Jesus."

She curled into his lap, her head on his chest. He took the time to feel the rhythm of her heart and hear her soft breathing. He forced himself to live in the moment and the incredible gift curled up in his lap.

Chapter Eleven

A late-October front had blown in and dropped the temperature. Wrapped up in Aunt Maggie's poncho, Lorrie Ann felt like Little Red Riding Hood as she followed the dirt road along the fence. Pulling the heavy wool closer, she grinned. Well, more like Purple Riding Hood. Sent to the Childress Ranch, Lorrie Ann carried a basket heavy with hot coffee and cinnamon rolls.

She slipped through the gate that divided the two properties and continued on the road until she saw the grand two-story limestone home. She remembered hiding in the huge house when she was little and recalled the broken boards leading to the sagging porch and the ugly carpet that gave the house a moldy smell.

Now, standing out against the majestic hills in the background, the porch and upper-level deck gleamed with newly replaced rich wood, taking the home back to the pride of the first Childress that had settled here.

As she moved closer, she saw John's truck parked at the side of the house, breaking the illusion of days gone by.

Taking a deep breath, she moved up the recently rebuilt steps. At the door, she hesitated with disappointment when she spotted two other vehicles. She shook her head. She should be relieved John had company. The less time they spent alone the better.

"Hello?" Stepping into the house was a shock. The place stood gutted; only a few of the old columns remained. From the front door, she could see all the way through the house to the French doors and huge window covering the back wall. Clear plastic covered old wood floors. Jake and two other men she recognized from church worked in the far left corner.

"Lorrie Ann." Jake turned off the power tool and walked toward her. "Let me guess—you're looking for John?"

She felt her face heat up, and she glanced to the grand staircase. John appeared at the top and paused when he spotted her. Then a grin filled his face, bringing out his dimple. She forgot all about Jake and the others.

"John! You have company, and I think she brought gifts from Maggie's kitchen." Jake took the loaded basket from her and peeked inside.

Now she knew why Aunt Maggie had packed so much. "With the front moving in so fast, she thought you might want some warm coffee. And of course, being Aunt Maggie, she had to send food, too."

In a few seconds, the guys pulled together makeshift chairs and passed around the basket. She found herself sitting on the foot of the curved stairs next to John.

There was no talking as the men ate the cinnamon rolls, just a few moans of appreciation. When George wiped his hands on paint-stained work jeans, she remembered the wipes in the basket and handed them out.

"This is why we work for you, John—the off chance your neighbor will feed us." Jake winked at her as he stood. "I guess that's good for a bit more work. We're going to finish the drywall in the kitchen, then it'll be ready for the cabinets." He nodded to Lorrie Ann and grinned. "Thanks for the delivery. It hit the spot."

"Want a tour?" John stood and offered his hand to her.

"It looks a little different from the last time I was here." She put her hand in his, enjoying the feel of his warmth and strength.

Her feminist friends in L.A. would be appalled at the way she liked feeling feminine and a bit fragile. Even though she knew safe and protected was an illusion. She sighed. Yep, she definitely needed to get back to California.

He led her to the area where the guys hung drywall. The nail gun punctured the wall with a loud thud.

"This is obviously the kitchen. We're putting a large island here that has a curved countertop raised on that side." He swung his arms, showing the layout. "It'll be large enough to fit five people. The stove will be here so you can face the living area while cooking. I thought about putting the sink there, too." He turned to face the back wall, where a giant window framed a view of the hills. "But I decided to keep it under the window looking out back. We're using local granite." He patted Jake on the back as they passed him. "Good work, guys. I can't thank you enough for helping me on your day off."

"Make sure to put in a good word for us with the man upstairs," Adrian said, wrapping a cord around another power tool as he started packing them up. "I love restoring the old homes around here."

John nodded. "I can't wait until we get started on the cabinets." He looked at Lorrie Ann. "We're using the old wood from the carriage house.

"Over in the far corner, where the large bay window sits, is a new room and bath." He placed his hand under her elbow. "For now, I'm going to use it as an office, but I wanted to have a bedroom on the ground floor if we ever need it." He gave her a lopsided grin. "I was thinking more along the lines of Dub moving in with us, but with Rachel's leg I think it's a good idea to have the bedroom option down here."

She nodded. When she and Brent had looked at houses,

it had never crossed their minds to think of the future or the needs of others. "That's a smart plan."

"This whole floor will remain open from the kitchen to the living room, with a large dining-room table along those windows joining the two." His words created an image of the perfect family living space. "A little like Maggie's." He winked at her. "I love her big table and the idea of family and friends always having a seat."

Lorrie Ann couldn't help comparing it against her life with Brent. The large glass-and-steel table at his house had such a different purpose, to impress and intimidate.

"That's perfect. Are you going to have it made out of the old wood?"

"No, I already have the table. On a mission trip to Mexico, we came across some furniture makers. They had this twelve-foot table. The legs are a foot thick and hand carved. They're incredible. The wood was saved from an old mission. The men were so proud of their work." He laughed. "We had to tie it down on the top of the bus with ropes running across the roof, crisscrossing from window to window."

His hand slipped from her elbow to her hand as he pulled her up the staircase. "The stairs and front porch were the first structures we repaired. It was amazing no one was hurt."

She laughed. "I used to hide here. The stairs scared me."

"No one's lived here for over twenty years. We had to evict a family of raccoons." With his last words, they reached the second floor. To the right, the large bay seating area drew her to step into the open space. The floor-to-ceiling window gave a panoramic view. From up here she could see her uncle's pecan orchard. The river curved below the bluff behind the house. She turned to John. "This is beautiful. You have a million-dollar view here."

He looked to the hallway behind him. "This floor had six small rooms and one bathroom. We reframed it as four rooms with larger closets and two-and-a-half baths. The front is the master."

She poked her head into each room. "Have the girls picked out their rooms yet?"

"Oh, yes. Celeste wants the room with the box-seat window. She likes the idea of hiding things in the seat, and it's next to my room. Rachel took the room with its own half bath."

She smiled, picturing Celeste with clothes, books and toys all over the floor and every piece of furniture. Rachel would have a place for everything and everything in its place.

"This is going to be a wonderful home for the girls."

"I'm hoping to get enough done that we can move in before May so Maggie can have her biggest cabin back for the summer tourists. Plus, it'll be nice to have our own place. Only one floor left." Going back to the large bay window, he led the way up a narrow staircase taking them to the once-upon-a-time attic.

"This is my favorite room." The large half-circle windows at the end of the room were breathtaking. "I won't be able to finish it out anytime soon, but I want the basics in place." He stood at the window that looked across the ranch. "From here you can see Dub's stables and arena."

He turned back to her, the sun highlighting his bone structure. She put her hand in her pocket to keep it from running along his jaw. The dark shadow of a beard gave him the look of a rugged workingman, the kind of man who took care of his family.

"I thought about making this floor the master suite, but it's a bit disconnected from the rest of the house, and all this room would be wasted on one person."

"Do you think you'll ever remarry?" Did she just blurt that out? "Sorry, that was really personal."

"You take care of my girls, and I've given you the first tour of my home. Hopefully, we're friends enough to ask personal questions." He glanced at his watch. "If we're going to eat dinner before the art opening, we need to close up shop." He held his arm out to her.

As they headed out of the house, she realized he never answered her question.

Standing in front of the mirror, Lorrie Ann twisted back and forth. Maybe she should change. The heels might be a bit much for an art opening in Kerrville. But she loved the way the black velvet straps laced up her calves. She wore a knee-length wraparound skirt and a blue-and-green-marbled silk shirt with a bit of a Southwest look to it. She glanced back in her closet. Maybe the shirt with a pair of jeans and a pair of Aunt Maggie's designer cowboy boots would be better.

A knock on the door interrupted her thoughts.

"Lorrie Ann?" Aunt Maggie's voice drifted through the door. "Pastor John's here."

Lorrie Ann's eyes flew to the clock by her bedside. Ugh, where had the time gone? She crossed the room and opened the door.

"Are the shoes too much?"

"You're asking me after what you wore to the Wednesday-night prayer meeting?" Laughter laced her voice. "Come on. You're beautiful, and that poor man looks nervous."

"Oh, Aunt Maggie, I'm sorry I didn't even think about how my choices affect you."

"Don't be silly. I don't let what others do or think bother me. Anyways, this is Texas. You can wear stilettos or torn jeans, as long as you walk with enough confidence. Now, hurry on with you."

Lorrie Ann took a deep breath and walked down the hallway, keeping her back straight. *Smile, stand tall and fake it as long as you have to.*

John stood with his back to them, looking at the photos lining the shelves.

Uncle Billy put the newspaper down and smiled at her. "Lorrie Ann, you look downright pretty."

John spun on his heels. "Wow, you always seem to surprise me."

"Is that a good thing?" She held her smile, trying to read him. "I wasn't sure what kind of art gallery we were going to, so if I need—"

"No, it's perfect. He does contemporary Western type of stuff, so I think you're perfect. I mean your outfit is perfect. Well, you are, too, but I..."

Her smile became real as her heart jumped around a little.

"Have her home by nine o'clock." Uncle Billy's stern voice startled them both.

A panicked look flashed across John's face. "The show doesn't end until—"

Uncle Billy laughed. "I'm just kidding. It's been a long time since I got to say that for one of my girls. Y'all be careful."

"Yes, sir." John shook his hand.

Lorrie Ann bit her lip as they headed out the door. The words *one of my girls* hit her heart hard and caused strange emotions to bubble up.

John tilted his head and gave her a questioning look. She managed to nod. "He... I don't think he's ever called me his girl before."

John's concern melted into a slow smile. "He loves you."

"I'm not even related to him by blood, and he's so quiet I never really knew how he felt. My mother dumped me on them and left." She crossed her arms around her waist and took in the pale yellows and pinks settling over the endless rows of pecan trees. She had never told anyone how she had come to live with her aunt. "I was in and out of their house growing up. My mom...well, she had issues. Whenever it got too rough or she got in over her head with the latest boyfriend, we would come here to hide." She looked up at John, and the warmth in his eyes pushed at the cold that had been in her heart for so long. No other man had ever listened to her the way he did. In a way, it scared her to find she might actually trust him. He didn't know the real Lorrie Ann. "When I was twelve she decided I got in her way and took off without a backward glance. That was the last time I saw her. Uncle Billy and Aunt Maggie didn't have a choice. They were stuck with me." She paused. "All these years later and they are still stuck with me. No one seems to know where my mom is—" she gave a half laugh "—or they're just not telling me."

Silence hung between them for a moment as John intently studied her face, his lips tight.

Finally he smiled. "That's not the story they tell. You were a blessing to a couple that had dreamed of having a house full of kids but were only able to have one. William's the kind of man who shows his love through action. Giving you a place to live, feeding you and taking care of you… That's him saying he loves you."

She used the tip of her finger to wipe away the tear before it fell and messed up her makeup. "I thought he just tolerated me because of Aunt Maggie."

"He may be quiet, but he loves his family deeply, and you are his family."

He paused at the end of the patio. "So, do we go in my well-loved, well-worn truck or your fancy city-slicker car?"

"I love your truck, but have you ever driven a BMW?"

With his eyes on the car, he gave a shake of his head.

She pulled the keys from her small clutch purse and held them up. "She's all yours tonight."

"Really?" Another smile slowly eased its way across his face, and she knew then and there she would do anything just to see his smile.

He sat behind the wheel and ran his hands over the leather steering wheel. She shook her head. What was it about men and cars?

Starting the engine, he eased the Beemer out of the driveway and winked at her. "I've never sat in, let alone driven, a machine worth more than I could make in three or more years as a country preacher."

"Well, enjoy. I'm trading it in for something more practical. It was a birthday gift from Brent. He said it would look good parked in front of our house when we got married." She watched the trees flash by as they climbed higher into the hills. "Since I won't be moving back I should get rid of the car, too."

"When do you plan on going back?"

"I'm not sure. A few things have to be cleared before I return. If it doesn't work out, I might just stay here for a while."

"A great deal of people would love for you to stay."

She laughed and made a face at him. "Yeah, right. Everything I worked for is back in L.A. It would be like…I don't know…letting Brent win."

"If you're happy, you win no matter where you live."

"I just can't imagine my life without everything I have in L.A. It's who I am now." She studied the sun setting behind the hills. Spots of red and yellow fall foliage mixed with the evergreens that covered the rocky slopes.

What scared her most? She could see herself in John's house, at his dinner table, watching the girls as they did their homework, hosting an all-girls sleepover while he hid upstairs in the master bedroom. She could see it so clearly and knew it was wrong. She didn't belong in his home, playing mother to his children. The sooner she got back to her real life the better for everyone.

"Is it safe to go back?"

She bit her lip. "You mean Brent? He's in rehab right now, and I won't go back unless I know he won't be around. If he stays in the band, I'll find another band to manage. I have enough connections and already have some people contacting me."

His jaw flexed, and he nodded, giving her a stiff smile before looking back to the road. "Good."

Good. That was all he could come up with to say? He shook his head. Just the thought of her being anywhere near that guy raised his blood pressure.

He knew the bruise on her eye didn't have anything to do with the accident. He took a deep breath and focused on the road, sliding the car around a sharp curve that hugged the hillside. This road had never felt so smooth.

Which just took his thoughts right back to Lorrie Ann, causing him to smile. She would have been just fine coming in his truck or her little show car. She might like to think of herself as all L.A., but she was also one of the most down-to-earth women he knew. He really enjoyed being in her company.

He cut a glance at his passenger, who stared out the window. He had gotten too personal earlier. *God, help me here. I haven't been on a date in a long time.* He tightened his fingers around the leather as they hugged another curve.

"Have you eaten at Mamasita's?"

She turned her head and smiled back at him. "Uncle Billy took us there anytime we had something to celebrate. It's his favorite restaurant." She gave a small laugh. "I love watching them make the tortillas."

"That always keeps Celeste entertained for a good fifteen minutes."

The conversation moved from the girls to his plans for the ranch house. A couple times he wanted to bring up her mother but wasn't sure how without breaking Sonia's trust. By the time they pulled into the parking lot of the restaurant, they had started discussing the Christmas pageant and ideas Lorrie Ann wanted to try.

Through dinner, they continued talking about pleasant things, when he really wanted to ask why she was going

back to a life that made her miserable. He sighed and reminded himself he didn't want a long-term relationship. It
was just one date.

As they left the restaurant and headed to the gallery, Lorrie Ann reminded herself she had been invited to come along
tonight because he didn't want to go alone.

This was not a real date.

A man like John would only invite her because she made
an uncomplicated companion. She grunted at the idea of her
being uncomplicated. A better word would be *convenient*.

By the time they arrived at the art gallery, she had any
wild idea of a romantic relationship firmly locked down.
They were friends. God sent her to Clear Water to reconnect with her faith. What better friend than John, a man of
God, to guide her?

He held out his arm as they approached the steps to a large
Victorian mansion. A hand-carved sign proclaimed the estab-
lishment as J. K. West's Fine Art Gallery and Studio.

The deep porch wrapped around the entire house. Elab-
orate iron lanterns hung from each column, and more light
blazed from the windows, welcoming them into its histori-
cal splendor.

The glass-and-wood door swung open as soon as her heels
clicked on the polished wooden boards. The well-dressed
hostess handed them a brochure about the artist and escorted
them to a buffet table full of hors d'oeuvres and desserts.
With a big smile, she offered them something to drink then
headed back to the door.

John leaned in close to her ear. "Between your car and
fancy shoes, I think they believe we're buyers."

She saluted him with her glass of ice water and gave him
a cheeky grin. "Maybe we are."

"Yeah, right." He glanced at a price listed next to a large

canvas. "Do you know how many vacuum cleaners I could buy for the price of one of Gary's paintings?"

Lorrie Ann gave a soft laugh. This man would be so easy to love. They moved through the rooms connected by large archways, each wall displaying another canvas.

"These are brilliant." Taking her gaze off the painting in front of them, she turned to John. "How do you know the artist?"

"We grew up playing football together until my grandparents took me to Houston my junior year. He moved in with me while he attended the Art Institute of Houston."

A hand grasped John's shoulder. They both turned quickly. "*I* played football. He just wanted to talk to the cheerleaders."

"Gary!" The men hugged and gave each other a pounding on the shoulder. "Where have you been hiding?"

"Some collectors wanted a tour of the studio upstairs." He turned to Lorrie Ann. She could not imagine this tall, lean man playing football. *Beautiful* came to mind with his dark hair framing perfect skin and teeth. His thick lashes gave the illusion of eyeliner, making his coffee-dark eyes riveting.

John moved into her line of vision, drawing her attention back to him. "Lorrie Ann, this is Gary Sanchez. Gary, Lorrie Ann is my neighbor's niece. She's visiting from Los Angeles."

He held out his hand to her. "Thank you so much for coming."

Lorrie Ann could not shake the feeling she had seen him somewhere before. "This sounds lame—" she smiled "—but have you done print work or TV? You look very familiar."

He shook his head, but John interrupted before he could speak.

"You've seen him in the wedding picture in the cabin."

Gary then shot a quick glance to Lorrie Ann with brows raised.

Lorrie Ann felt her face grow warm. "I'm watching the

girls." She swallowed, suddenly feeling nervous. "Rachel broke her leg."

Gary laughed and slapped John on the back again. "Yeah, John told me what happened. So, you're the one who's helping out?" His beautiful smile showed off perfect teeth.

Lorrie Ann smiled back.

John took a sip of his water. "Gary *was* my best man."

"I'm still your best man."

"This summer Gary's moving into the former maids' quarters. He's turning it into a studio."

"I prefer to call it the guesthouse." He glanced around the room and smiled at a couple studying his work. "I'm excited about living in the Hill Country." He nodded toward the archway to their right. "Have you been to the front parlor yet?"

"No, we were heading that way."

"Your work is breathtaking. The strokes of colors are so packed with emotion and energy they pull me into the painting."

"Thank you."

As they stepped into the room, a four-by-six canvas pulled her closer. "Wow. This is…" She stared at the painting. "It's so uplifting, like there's music coming right off the image."

John turned to Gary. "Is this what you did with the pictures of Celeste and me?"

"This is *Joy* number 3. I listened to your CD while I painted. A total of five paintings came from those photos and drawings from that day."

Lorrie Ann tilted her head and squinted. In the swirl of vibrant colors, she could see a larger figure swinging a smaller one through the space above him, each brushstroke sweeping her along. "You and Celeste posed for this painting?"

John grinned. "Not really. Gary came out to visit last summer to do some landscape studies."

Gary chuckled. "While I worked on sketches, Celeste grew a little bored, so John started spinning her in circles. I ended up taking more pictures of them than the landscape. By the time I got back to the studio, I knew I had to capture that joy on canvas." He turned back to the painting. "I've already sold two. They've become my favorites."

"Celeste will love to see this."

"They're on my website. Numbers 2 and 5 are in New Mexico." He placed his hand on John's shoulder. "I'm so glad you made it. I've got to play host and sell some of my babies. Very nice meeting you, Lorrie Ann, and I hope to see you again before you head back to L.A."

They moved to another room, studying a collection of smaller paintings grouped on one wall.

Lorrie Ann chuckled. John raised an eyebrow. "What's so funny?"

"Only in Texas would two high-school football players become an artist and a preacher." Her gaze met his. "How did you end up a pastor?"

What she really wanted to ask him? How did a drop-dead-gorgeous hunk become a country pastor in the middle of nowhere? But she knew that would come across as shallow.

"In the church I attended as a teenager there were two youth ministers that changed my life. I knew my purpose by the time I finished high school. I was called to serve God."

"Wow, it was that clear and easy?" She followed him to the next painting.

He looked down at the glass of water he held between his hands. Raising his eyes back to her, he pulled one corner of his mouth to give her a lopsided grin.

"I have to admit it's a bit more complicated. I grew up in Flower Mound, outside Dallas. That's where Gary and I played football. My junior year I lost my parents. They were flying to an air show with my uncle and aunt when their plane went down."

Lorrie Ann moved closer to John, no longer interested in the artwork surrounding them. She laid her hand on his arm.

"I found myself living with my grandparents in Houston." He gave a grunt and took another drink of his ice water. "Grieving four family members, they didn't know what to do for a confused sixteen-year-old. They dropped me off in the youth building at their church, a megachurch with programs that kept me busy day and night. I joined the worship band and found a place I belonged."

She knew what it felt like to be dumped and alone. Of course, her mother had had a choice. His focus stayed on the painting in front of them, but Lorrie Ann wondered if he even saw the room. After a few minutes of silence, she searched for a safe topic.

"You played in a band? Gary mentioned a CD." She grinned. "Now, that sounds right up my alley. Do you write? What instrument did you play?"

He started walking to the next wall display. "If it had strings I played it, guitar being my favorite. The music is part of my past. Chuck and Cody, my youth ministers, had a huge impact on my life and growing my relationship with God. When I graduated, there was never a doubt that I wanted to serve God and join the ministry."

"I wish I had that kind of faith."

"You can. We're designed to worship, but with free will we get to choose who or what we worship."

"I think I might have been at the wrong altar for the past twelve years."

He leaned into her, lightly bumping her shoulder. "It happens to the best of us. I understand how easy it is to have the wrong god on your altar and not even know it." He sat on a flat cushioned bench in the middle of the room and contemplated a landscape that covered the wall from floor to ceiling.

"Don't let guilt or fear stop you from living a full life." His eyes never moved from the painting.

How did he sound so confident and nonjudgmental at the

same time? "You make it sound so easy." She slid down next to him.

"Oh, it's not easy." He turned to gaze into her eyes. "It can be so hard sometimes you just want to hide."

"I can see you leading a huge congregation, so how did you end up in little ol' Clear Water?"

"God knew what my family needed before I did. Carol had talked about moving back before she died." His hands braced on the edge of the bench, he dropped his head and paused for a minute. After a deep breath, he continued, "After we lost her, it became difficult to be around our friends, the sad looks and the awkwardness when they celebrated good news. Dub had been trying to get me to his church for about a year. The old pastor wanted to retire, and they couldn't find a full-time replacement."

"Pastor Kemp." She snapped her fingers and smiled as she remembered the old man. "He baptized me. I thought he was in his eighties back then."

"Yeah, that's him. He's incredible."

She thought about how she had lived her life, but she couldn't imagine what she had to offer. "I don't know how God could use me."

He smiled at her and winked. "He already has. Like organizing a Christmas pageant?"

She nudged him in the arm. "No fair."

"As Katy and Maggie have said over and over again, you came to us because God knew we needed you." He paused, tilted his head and looked her straight in the eye. "I think you needed us also."

She sighed, and her smile felt a little wobbly. "Oh, I know I needed all of you much more than you'll ever need me."

Lorrie Ann glanced at the large clock on the wall, surprised by the time. "It's late. We should be heading home. You're not going to be late for church in the morning. Everyone will blame me." She looked around the gallery and noticed most of the people had already left.

John took her arm to slow her down and laughed. "You act like the clock's about to strike midnight and your car will turn into a pumpkin." He looked around. "Let's say goodbye to Gary."

Lorrie Ann felt a flush cover her face. What was it about this man that caused her to act like a sixteen-year-old?

As they neared the front, she spotted Gary talking to a couple. John lightly touched his arm and said goodbye. Gary gave her a light hug and thanked them for coming.

With her hand on John's arm, they walked to her car. Lorrie Ann settled into the leather seat and studied John as the light from the dashboard reflected on his face. He had a purpose for his life and he knew it. His girls, the church, even his late wife knew the purpose. How did she ever think she could fit into his life?

Chapter Twelve

Wednesday night, sitting in the second pew, Lorrie Ann couldn't believe she had been back in Clear Water for over a week now. After Saturday's nondate, she'd been careful to keep it all business with John. She declined invitations to stay for dinner when he arrived home and avoided any contact with him.

Not that it stopped her from thinking of him. The affection she felt for the girls surprised her the most. Just the thought of saying goodbye to them already tore at her heart.

Lorrie Ann looked at the scriptures being read: *Don't let your hearts be troubled. Trust in God, and trust also in me. For our present troubles are small and won't last very long. Yet they produce for us a glory that vastly outweighs them and will last forever!*

She smiled as Celeste squirmed next to her, causing Rachel to shoot her little sister a warning look.

As people started sharing prayer requests and praises, Celeste raised her hand and waved it until her dad acknowledged her. "I would like to thank God for bringing Miss Lorrie Ann to us and pray that she stays." She looked at Lorrie Ann before adding, "God willing." With a nod, she folded her hands in her lap and lowered her head.

Lorrie Ann put her hand on Celeste's back and could feel her heart beat. Her chest tightened at the little girl's prayer. Rachel rolled her eyes. Lorrie Ann found herself smiling and adding her own prayers silently to the list. Soon, everyone stood and joined hands to finish the meeting in prayer.

Taking a deep breath, Lorrie Ann slung her bag over her shoulder. The people working with the pageant would meet in the fellowship hall tonight.

"Lorrie Ann!" Katy ran up to her, interlocking their arms. She pulled her close and kept walking toward the back door. "I'm so excited you are doing this. Martha was good, but it was the same thing for the past twenty years. If there is anything I can do, anything at all, please let me know."

Lorrie Ann smiled. Katy's enthusiasm gave her a shot of confidence. "Since you know the kids, I really need your help with them. Picking out the music, casting, that sort of thing."

"Oh, sure, that will be fun. I have some ideas I would love to run by you. Martha had the same songs every year."

As they walked into the hall, the smell of coffee already filled the air. Maggie once again stood behind the counter with a couple other women sorting the desserts.

Lorrie Ann organized the packets Aunt Maggie and Yolanda had helped her create. The room filled with adults, teens and children. She groaned when she saw Rachel sitting with Seth. "Rachel, come here, please."

With a heavy sigh and a roll of the eyes, Rachel stomped over to her. "We're just sitting there talking."

"Yes, but do you think your father would be okay with you sitting in the corner, alone with Seth?" She handed her a stack of color-coded folders. "Maybe Seth can help me pass these out? And I recommend you and Seth sit with your other friends."

John entered the room with Vickie by his side. She touched his arm and laughed. Lorrie Ann opened her computer and focused on the screen. She had no right to be angry about another woman talking with him. Her tongue started pushing back and forth against her teeth.

When she looked over the room, Vickie flashed a smile and leaned closer to John. He cleared his throat and stepped away, moving toward Lorrie Ann.

Oh, that felt good, even though she knew pettiness should be above her. She turned to smile at Vickie's narrowing eyes. Yes, she could be the bigger person.

John stood next to her. "Are you ready?"

She nodded to the people gathering around the tables. "Not sure if they're ready for me."

"They'll be fine." He gave her the slow smile that melted her heart. "Once this meeting gets started, I'll be taking the missionary committee to my office. Tonight shouldn't last as long. I might even get to take the girls home tonight."

Disappointment inundated her. She had started looking forward to the bedtime ritual. As a child, she'd never had a routine of any kind. She had been too busy staying out of the way.

John called for everyone's attention. "Welcome. First, I'm excited to announce that the play has been moved to the unfinished youth building."

Mutters and mumbles filled the room.

Vickie spoke up first. "Pastor John, that doesn't make any sense. There are no walls."

"We don't have electricity run to the building yet," someone else yelled from the back.

John grinned. "That's right. We're scheduled to have utilities in by the end of next week. As far as no walls, that works perfectly for the ideas Lorrie Ann has shared with me." He smiled at her. "Now, if you'll excuse me, I have another meeting. I leave you in capable hands."

Her stomach dropped a bit when he left. She scanned the room. Everyone had turned their attention to her. It surprised her a bit when she realized how many friendly faces sat in the crowd. Maybe her memories had painted the town much darker than it deserved.

Stretching her spine, she filled her lungs with oxygen and put her best smile on her face. Lorrie Ann slowly rose from her chair. "This year we will be using live animals and a cherry picker to hoist an angel in the air. The concrete floor with the metal poles will be a perfect stage for our setting."

Mrs. Miller, the Dragon Lady, hit her cane on the floor. "Live animals with kids and an audience? Sounds dangerous to me."

"What if it's cold or rains?" someone else shouted out.

Lorrie Ann continued to smile and made eye contact with the people gathered. It was a mix of people from six years old to eighty. "That's why I need help from you. We will need an animal wrangler. We'll also come up with an alternate plan in case of bad weather. When I asked Pastor John about the problems with the plan, he gave me some great advice. He said to proceed with faith." Lorrie Ann held up her green folder. "Based on the information Aunt Maggie gave me last week, I've created folders for each person by committee."

Rachel handed out the last folder and sat at the table with the other girls.

Lorrie Ann soaked in the level of excitement she heard in the conversation.

"I have ideas and drawings included in your folder, but please feel free to come up with your own."

"Wow, Lorrie Ann, this appears ambitious." Jake leafed through his folder and then smiled at her. "It looks great."

"The costumes are awesome."

Vickie stood with arms crossed. "We usually just redo and alter the ones we already have. Your plan will need new costumes. Who's paying for all this material?"

"We do have a small budget, and donations have already been made to cover the costs."

"I have some leftover panels we can use for the set design."

"Thank you, Adrian. Now, if you look at the first pages you'll see a calendar with rehearsal dates and deadlines. It's color coded to your folder. There's no need for everyone to be at every meeting or practice. Not until we start full runthroughs, anyway. And as groups you can set your times to meet as often as you need. We're going to need the youth group and children's choir to meet Saturday to confirm parts. There are twenty roles, plus the two choirs and band."

As they separated into groups, Katy, Rhody, Abby and Paul took the teens and children in order to assign roles.

Separated from the groups, a dark-haired boy sat alone in the far corner. He pounded out a beat on his legs with a pair of drumsticks. The piercings alone screamed *back off,* but with the black clothes and spiked hair he made sure everyone saw his contempt. Lorrie Ann smiled, thinking of the rebellious teen she had been. She approached him carefully and sat down, not talking to him at first. After a few minutes, she held out her hand to him. "Hello, I'm Lorrie Ann Ortega. Are you here to play in the band?"

"Nope. I brought Carlos." He stuck the sticks into his heavy army boots.

"Do you play?"

"Are you the lady that works with a band in L.A.?"

"Yep, that's me." She winked. "So, the hair and piercings are the norm where I come from."

He snorted. "They don't much like it here."

"Are you good with the drums, or do you just mess around?"

He shrugged.

"Well, I have an idea, but to make it work I need a really good drummer."

He pointed his chin toward the adult committees working on their piece of the show. "They would have a fit if you used me."

Lorrie Ann laughed. "Funny, I used those words myself

just a few days ago. I haven't been run out yet." She leaned closer to him. "I have it on good authority God does not love us based on our clothes or hairstyle."

He didn't respond.

"Thursday night, the band is getting together to go over the music. It'll only be the teens and their leaders. You should come by, and I can tell you more about my vision for a drum solo. The drummer will be the backbone of the whole show, so he has to do more than keep a beat."

"Kyle's not too bad. He's the only one with any skill. Don't know if he could carry a solo."

"It's not a part with the band."

One pierced eyebrow arched up, and she thought she might have seen a slight nod.

"I expect to see you." With the final word, she walked away, smiling.

Lorrie Ann moved through each group to answer questions and hear ideas. She loved the planning stage, seeing all the different parts coming together to make one great event. Jake and his crew had some plans of building a village with storefronts leading into a three-level platform she had drawn out.

The only group that seemed a little cold to the ideas was the sewing crew. Vickie kept complaining, but with Maggie on the committee, Lorrie Ann didn't have to deal with her directly, even though she kept trying to pull Lorrie Ann into an argument. Lorrie Ann just smiled and finally excused herself after giving them the amount donated to purchase new fabric. The look on Vickie's face brought a shallow pleasure to Lorrie Ann's inner teen.

John tried to stay focused on the missionary work and funds, but his thoughts kept floating back to Lorrie Ann. Saturday had been fun, and he got the impression she had enjoyed herself, too.

However, when he got home Tuesday after work, she had

been out the door before he removed his jacket. Tonight, at the family dinner, she had made a point of sitting at the opposite end of the table. He should be happy about the distance she put between them, but it had irritated him.

He knew she needed to heal and he…well, he didn't have anything to give to a personal relationship. He couldn't even be completely honest with her because of his promise to Sonia, her mother. Maybe he would get Sonia's number from Maggie.

He leaned back in his chair. Lorrie Ann made it so easy to talk. He couldn't remember the last time he had talked about his parents' deaths and the path that had brought him to the ministry.

Looking down at his notes, he tried to refocus and saw little swirls and stick people. At least he hadn't been reduced to doodling hearts and Lorrie Ann's name. He shook his head and checked his watch. The budget meeting would be over soon. He had started looking forward to his Wednesday-night chats with Lorrie Ann on the back porch.

An hour and a half later people started leaving.

The door suddenly swung open, and for a moment Lorrie Ann's brain couldn't comprehend what she saw. She looked around for help. Maggie and Yolanda worked the kitchen. Rachel, Seth and Celeste still sat at the table with Vickie. They all stopped to stare at the stranger.

Brent couldn't be here; he just couldn't. "You're in rehab" was all her brain could manage. How had Brent ended up in her church?

"Hello, Lorrie Ann." His Irish accent completed the charming facade of bright blue eyes and rumpled blond hair. "It was stupid. I don't have a problem like those other blokes."

"How did you find me?" She had to get him out of here.

"GPS on the Beemer. Had it installed, case it was stolen." He walked toward her, ignoring the people in the room. "Never dreamed I'd use it to track down my own sweetheart."

Maggie came across the room and stood in front of the six-foot Irishman, her hands on her hips. "I'm Margarita Ortega-Schultz, Lorrie Ann's aunt."

"Pleasure to meet ya." His brogue rolled off his tongue as his hand hung in the air, ignored. He stuffed it back in his jeans pocket and cleared his throat. "Well, I came to make things right."

Lorrie Ann found her voice. "You shouldn't have driven all this way. I don't want to talk to you."

Both of John's girls sat wide-eyed, glued to the drama in front of them. She saw Rachel stand, gripping her crutch. She had to get this ugliness away from them. She put her hands on Aunt Maggie's shoulders. "Could you take the girls home for me?"

She narrowed her eyes at Brent. "Yes." Her small frame stood tall as she took a step closer to Lorrie Ann's ex. "She has family here and friends to take care of her. Come, girls, I'll drive you home tonight." She waited for the girls to join her, and with them tucked under her arms she headed to the door.

Brent watched Maggie leave before turning back to Lorrie Ann. "Well, that was unpleasant. What did ya tell her?"

"Nothing, except I ended the engagement. You need to leave." She gathered her paperwork and prayed to have the right words and actions to send him away. "You'll have to go to Kerrville in order to find a hotel at this time of night."

"I'm not leaving until we talk about this."

Lorrie Ann stopped and glared at him. She stared at the man she had dreamed of building a life with in California. He didn't get it. For him it was all about money and fame. She had been caught up in that lifestyle, too. Now she looked at him and saw her past, a past she would no longer allow to weigh her down. "There is nothing to talk about, Brent. Now leave." She shoved her folders into her bag.

"I called, texted and emailed." Desperation edged his voice. "You wouldn't return any of them. I had to talk to you."

"I didn't return them because I *don't* want to talk to you. It's over. Go back to rehab and get your life straightened out."

He moved to her and fell to one knee. "Lorrie Ann, I know what I did was unforgivable, but it was the drugs, not me. I would never do that to you. In the past two years I have never raised a hand to ya."

She stood straight and looked him in the eye. "Leave, Brent. It's over."

"No, I'm not giving up until you agree to come home with me." He reached up to touch her face.

She stepped back and bit hard on her lip. "We're not together anymore, Brent, and it's more than just what happened that night. It's more than the drugs and partying. I don't want that lifestyle. I want more."

"More!" He shot up from the floor and grabbed her arms, pulling her against him. "The houses, the cars, all the clothes and parties aren't enough for you?"

Lorrie Ann tried to pull away from him, but he was too strong. She looked him in the eye. How did she ever think she loved this man? Without a doubt, she'd made the right decision leaving California. Fear started paralyzing her; she knew that would be the worst thing to let happen. How could she get him out of here without anyone getting hurt?

Chapter Thirteen

John glanced at his watch. The Christmas meeting should be over. He prayed for open hearts and minds to hear Lorrie Ann's ideas.

She had shared a great vision with him of how the pageant could look. With a sigh, he thought of all the times people fought him over change just because it was change.

"They've been running for a year now and doing well. I move we increase the monthly funds sent to Peru by fifty dollars."

John raised his eyebrows. He had missed the whole discussion. Everyone voted in agreement, and Deacon Copeland adjourned.

At a light knock on the door, they all turned. Vickie poked her head in the room.

"Pardon the intrusion, but there's trouble in the fellowship hall."

"Is someone hurt?" John moved to the door, his heart jumping a beat faster, thinking of Celeste and Rachel.

"Oh, no, it's an unexpected guest." She bit the corner of her mouth. "Brent Krieger, Lorrie Ann's fiancé."

He rushed down the hall not hearing anything else Vickie said. He needed to get to Lorrie Ann. The thought of her ex in the same room with her sent unfamiliar anger surging through his bloodstream.

Barging into the room, he didn't see anything but Lorrie Ann being pinned against a stranger, his large hands wrapped around her small arms.

"Get your hands off her!" John's voice was sharp and demanding.

The other man released her and took a step back. His glare moved back and forth between John and Lorrie Ann.

John noticed Yolanda outside the kitchen area with a frying pan clasped tightly in two hands. Seth stood, his fist clenched tight, a cell phone in one hand. Tension filled the room.

"I suggest you leave now."

"I don't know who you are, but she's mine, and this is between us."

"She is *not* your anything," John snarled, moving to stand next to Lorrie Ann. He was ready to physically remove this jerk if needed. He felt her hand softly lie against his arm and looked down. Her straight back and smile reassured him she could handle the situation.

Brent's accented voice broke their contact. "Lorrie Ann, come back with me. I don't want to lose the life we have there."

"You don't get it, Brent. I don't want more of what we had. I want more family, community, a real purpose for my life. I need God in my life."

The door eased open, and Jake, in his uniform, slipped into the room.

Brent's gaze darted from person to person, and his hands started to shake. "I promise to stay in rehab, Lorrie Ann. I'm getting better. I realized how important you are in my life. I want to fix us. I want to go back to what we had. I need your forgiveness so we can start over."

John watched her intensely, tracking the emotions that

fluttered across her features one at a time. He prayed, without taking his eyes off her face, that God would wrap her tightly in His love and let her know she didn't stand alone.

Lorrie Ann squeezed his arm with a barely there touch. Her soft low voice broke the profound silence. "Thank you, Brent." A gentle smile eased its way to her eyes. "I do forgive you."

A big smile covered the Irishman's face as he took a step toward her. John stiffened.

Lorrie Ann raised her hands, palms out. "No, Brent, I forgive you because I need to in order to move forward. We're finished. You need to leave now. Everything that needed to be said has been said." Chin up, she took a step back, closer to John. "Goodbye."

John didn't like the man's clenched fists. Brent tried to loom over Lorrie Ann and brought one hand up to point a finger at her. "You will regret this. You'll lose your job, and no one will hire you. Your career will be over. See where your God is then."

Hand resting on his gun, Jake opened the door wide and stepped back with one brow raised. Brent shot a heated glare around the room before he stomped out and slammed the door.

Silence fell heavily in the fellowship hall. John slid an arm over her shoulders. "Are you all right?"

She took a deep breath and nodded. Her small frame trembled.

From the corner, Vickie demanded everyone's attention. "I told you she doesn't belong. Her history with men has reared its ugly head. Deacons, Pastor John—" she edged closer to Lorrie Ann, jabbing the air with her finger "—I'm asking that you ban her. I'll direct the pageant."

The three older men shuffled and looked to John with uncomfortable expressions.

Yolanda crossed the room to block Vickie's path. "She

doesn't have a history. You made it up. You lied, and I let you. This time I'm not going to let you chase her out of town. This is her home, too."

Vickie gasped, her mouth opening and closing. Her heavy breathing filled the air. "But she…"

Jake positioned himself next to Vickie. "That's enough. In high school we all stayed silent. It stops tonight, Vickie. We're adults now. It's time to grow up." He looked Lorrie Ann in the eye. "I'm sorry for not speaking up when the rumors grew."

Seth left the corner and grabbed his mother's hand. "Mom, let's go, please."

"But I… She…" Vickie pointed to Lorrie Ann. "She doesn't have a right to be here. I didn't…"

John stepped toward Vickie and prayed for the right way to handle the situation. He forced his jaw to relax, wanting to defend Lorrie Ann but knowing he also had to be Vickie's pastor. Anger and bitterness surrounded Vickie.

"Vickie, gossip and rumors have no place in the church." He stopped a few feet away from her and put his hand on Seth's shoulder. The boy's face burned red, and he kept his eyes down. "I know this has been a brutal year for you, but turning on others isn't the answer."

Seth glanced at him from under long bangs. He turned to his mother. "Mom. Please, can we just leave?"

Jake held out his arm. "Come on. I'll make sure you get home safe." He glanced at Lorrie Ann. "I'll call the sheriff and see that Brent gets all the way out of town."

With a glance filled with resentment, Vickie allowed her son and Jake to pull her from the room.

The three deacons lingered by the opposite door, ready to make a quick exit. "Well, um…it's late. We should be going. Call us if you need anything, Pastor." They each nodded to the women. "Night, Yolanda. Lorrie Ann."

Yolanda's gentle voice bid them a good night.

Lorrie Ann sat alone, her bag pulled close, not saying a word.

As soon as the men closed the door behind them, she turned to Yolanda. "Yolanda, thank you. After dealing with Brent, I didn't know what to say to Vickie. Thanks for standing up for me."

Yolanda rushed to her side, sitting next to her. "Oh, Lorrie Ann, I'm so sorry it was twelve years too late. I should've done that back in high school. I was so afraid of her, and, well, jealousy is just ugly."

Lorrie Ann's forehead went into deep wrinkles, and her gaze jumped to Yolanda's face. "Jealousy? Why would *you* be jealous of me?"

The younger woman laughed and pulled Lorrie Ann close. In that moment, she resembled her mother. "It's really lame, but I thought my mom loved you more. At school, you were so cool, and the teachers would always compare my work to yours. Then there was your singing."

"How sad are we? I always felt like an intruder." Lorrie Ann tucked her hair behind her ears. "Remember when we were little and told each other all our secrets?"

Yolanda took her cousin's hand in hers. Her voice dropped to a whisper. "I'm so sorry I wasn't there for you. Especially when Vickie spread those ugly lies. You couldn't even trust me enough to let me know what's been going on the past few weeks."

"I've handled everything wrong." Lorrie Ann used the pad of her thumb to wipe a tear off Yolanda's cheek. "Tell you what. I'll forgive our teenage drama if you forgive me for discounting our friendship all these years."

Yolanda pulled Lorrie Ann close again. "I don't deserve your forgiveness."

"The stories Vickie told about me in high school might have been lies, but the choices I've made since are all mine." Lorrie Ann pulled away from Yolanda.

John watched her move across the room to gather up supplies. With his elbows on his knees, he rested his chin in the palm of his hand. He still needed to battle down his own anger at the attacks both Brent and Vickie had brought into the church. He didn't trust himself to speak right now, so he continued to listen and pray.

With her back turned to him, her voice sounded muffled, but he could still hear the uncertainty. "Coming here might have been a mistake. Church has never seemed like a good place for me to be."

John sat up, unable to allow that comment to go unchallenged. "Lorrie Ann, the church should be a place of refuge, a safe corner in a world of devastating storms. What happened here tonight had nothing to do with God, but you handled both with grace. This church belongs to you as much as anyone else. You belong to God. Can you forgive us?" He stood in front of her now, wanting to take her in his arms.

"Us? You didn't have anything to do with it." Her eyes looked huge as she gazed up at him.

"You've had so many arrows thrown at your heart. I shouldn't have allowed it to happen tonight."

Lorrie Ann smiled. "You can't be everywhere all the time. I'm thinking about the scripture you gave Aunt Maggie to read tonight. It said our troubles are small and won't last forever. But they give us glory in the long run." Lorrie Ann reached for Yolanda's hand. "I faced my monsters tonight and realized they are just hurt people. For twelve years I've been running. No more."

Yolanda hugged her. "I've missed you." A cell phone went off in the kitchen. "Oh, that's Mom's ringtone." Yolanda rushed to answer her phone. "Hey, Mom, Lorrie Ann's fine. Yeah, he's gone." She looked to John and Lorrie Ann. "I'm with John and Lorrie Ann now." She smiled and nodded to whatever Maggie said on the other end. "Okay, I'll tell her. Love you."

"So what did Aunt Maggie say?" Lorrie Ann asked.

"Apparently, Rachel and Celeste are worried about you and waiting for their story."

John had his phone out to call the girls.

"I came with Mom, so I need a ride to my place."

Pulling the keys from her bag, Lorrie Ann handed them to Yolanda. "Here, take my car, and I'll ride to the house with John."

John walked to the door. "Sounds like a plan. The girls are anxious to see Lorrie Ann."

Yolanda followed them out and waited as John locked the building.

"I'll see you tomorrow. I love you, Yolanda."

"Yeah, me, too." Yolanda wrapped her in a hug before getting in the little sports car.

John held open his passenger door and waited for Lorrie Ann to buckle up. They watched as the BMW backed out and drove down Main Street before heading home.

Driving over Second Crossing, John's thoughts were still centered around Lorrie Ann. She came across as strong, but there was vulnerability at her core that made him want to protect her. She had not had many people to trust in her life, starting with her mother. To be that man for her scared him. He had let Carol down. She had deserved a better husband than the one he was to her. He hadn't been able to protect his wife. What worm in his brain made him think he could do any better for Lorrie Ann?

He thought of Lorrie Ann's mother. Sonia was afraid of disappointing her daughter after years of struggling with alcohol and drugs. She had made Maggie and him promise not to tell Lorrie Ann about her going through rehab in San Antonio. She was just an hour away and afraid to see her daughter. Maybe he had something in common with her. They both were cowards. He gave a short laugh.

"What?"

He shook his head and grinned at her. "Nothing. Just thinking."

John pulled in front of his cabin and cut the engine, but instead of getting out, they both stared at the dark landscape surrounding the cabin in silence. He wanted to give her some extra time to calm her nerves. To be honest, he really wanted to wrap her in his arms and protect her from the ugliness of the world.

"Thank you, John. I like to pretend I'm strong and independent, but I felt much safer when you charged into the room." She looked out the side window, her fingers playing with the handle but not opening the door.

"You *are* strong and independent. Doesn't mean you don't need support."

The porch light came on, and Aunt Maggie stepped outside, peering into the darkness.

John laughed. "I feel like a teenager bringing home his date." He turned to her. "Ready?"

With a nod, she climbed out of his truck. He followed her, grinning as she marched straight to his room, where the girls waited. She barely stopped for a quick hug with her aunt.

Maggie laid a hand on his arm. "Is she okay? I've been praying nonstop since I left with the girls."

He nodded. "You'd be proud." He smiled down at the fierce prayer warrior. "God works in strange ways."

"Yes, He does."

John leaned against the railing. "Have you told her about her mother yet?"

"No." She sighed and shook her head. "Sonia's afraid. I told her Lorrie Ann could handle it, but you know how guilt eats at people."

"The longer we keep it from her, the more betrayed she's going to feel."

Maggie laid a hand on his shoulder. "I know. I'll talk to Sonia again. With Lorrie Ann in town, there is no excuse."

She sighed and patted him on the shoulder. "It's been a long day. Good night."

"Night, Maggie."

A little bit later, the door eased open, and Lorrie Ann's head poked through. "Ah, there you are. Not sure if you had gone to bed yet."

He spent a moment just watching her move next to him before speaking. The cool breeze pushed her dark curls from her face. "The girls got their princess story?"

She cut her gaze to him for a quick second before going back to the stars. "Yeah, thanks for letting me tuck them in. Who would have guessed the highlight of my week would be a bedtime fairy tale?"

"The smallest things in life can be the biggest blessings."

"I think I'm starting to see that." She rubbed her hands together and tucked them under her arms. "I'll come by in the morning and help with breakfast." She raised her eyebrows and smiled. "Give you time to shave in peace."

"Ah, yes, the little things." He walked her across the graveled path to Maggie's back door.

She paused as she reached for the screen door and looked up at him. "Well, good night."

John swallowed hard and stared into her large eyes, the color dancing from gray to green. Then he remembered to mumble, "Good night."

He wanted to lean in and kiss her, but he took a step back instead and shoved his hands in his pockets. With one last smile, she turned and disappeared into the dark kitchen. John really needed a distraction. Tossing a green Jolly Rancher into his mouth, he headed back to the cabin.

Chapter Fourteen

John frowned as he thought about the unused guitars and violins he had in storage. For a Saturday, the church teemed with an unusual number of people. Music poured from the sanctuary. Now the loud enthusiastic chords filled the church with joy, even the misplaced and out-of-tune ones. They could use some good instruments.

"Um…Pastor John, I…um…" Rhody scratched the back of his neck as he stepped out of one of the small rooms, blocking John's path. "I was wondering if I could ask you something."

"Sure, Rhody, how can I help you?" John bit back a smile as he watched the other man fidget and look everywhere else to avoid eye contact.

"Well, the other day Katy…um, wanted to talk to you about our marriage. Do you remember?"

"I remember. Have y'all gone to one of the counselors I told you about?" Dread filled John. He didn't want to give out marriage advice.

"No, I don't think… Well, they don't know us…." Rhody made a sound in his throat. "I just want to make her happy. She seems fine one moment, and then she's sad. She's always moping over these travel magazines, and I think about the

crazy stories of women just taking off, no warning. I'm…
I'm afraid one day she's gonna leave."

"Maybe she just wants to travel. Where have y'all gone
on vacation?" Regret swamped him as John thought of the
vacation Carol had taken without him.

"Vacation? With the store open seven days a week, I don't
have time."

John closed his eyes. The same excuse he'd given Carol
every time she'd planned time together. *God, You know I
hate giving marriage advice. Please help me say what he
needs to hear.* "What about your honeymoon? Where did
you take her?"

"We went to San Antonio. It was the Stockshow and
Rodeo. My brother got Grand Champion Steer that year."

Stopping himself from rolling his eyes, John put his hand
on Rhody's shoulder. "Listen, she wants to share an adventure with you. Let her pick a place to go then take her. Enjoy
the gift God's given you."

"You think that's all it is? She wants a vacation with me?"

"She loves you. Those four boys are her world. But sometimes we can feel our world is too small."

Rhody smiled. "I can do that. It'll be hard covering the
store, but maybe my parents can step in for a bit, or Vickie.
Yeah, I can do this." He clasped John's shoulder. "Thank
you."

John took a deep breath as he watched his friend head out
the church door with a new joy in his step. He thought of the
simple things he'd never get to do for Carol. Regret made his
shoulders heavy.

He continued to the sanctuary, hoping to hear the band
practice. As he walked through the doors, only silence filled
the space. Checking his watch, he frowned. He had missed
them.

Walking up front to the stage, he saw one of the old church

guitars resting on its stand. He picked it up and played a few chords.

He thought of Rhody and the store. It was so easy to let people down. The hours he had put into his music had destroyed his marriage. Putting the guitar down, he walked to the piano and sat, looking over the sheet music.

Without thought, his fingers started dancing across the keys. Lorrie Ann brought the best out in the kids. Images of Lorrie Ann faded into memories of Carol working with the youth at his old church. He flinched when his fingers hit the wrong chord.

He had taken Carol and his family for granted. His jaw locked. Worse, he had avoided responsibility by blaming the music God had given him. He had told Rhody to savor the gift of love. What a hypocrite.

Did he deserve another chance at love? Muscle memory took over, and his fingers flew across the keys. The music he had kept locked up poured out of each individual cell inside him, and he surrounded himself in the emotions emptied from every note.

As Lorrie Ann headed back to the sanctuary, it surprised her to hear a piano. The carpeted hall silenced her footsteps. As she approached, the music started soft, drifting down the hall. The tone changed, and passion filled the air, rising high and swirling in a storm of chaos and fear. Then it quieted down again, a feeling of sweet hope in each note. That could not be one of the kids; it sounded too professional even on the ancient piano. She froze in the doorway.

John sat, fingers on the worn keys, absorbed in the music he created. Locks of hair moved as his head dipped down then thrust back, eyes closed tight.

The composition compelled her to move toward him. Energy and worship filled the empty pews. The disappearing sun reached through the colored glass, highlighting the man at the piano in a wave of rich color.

It all came to a sudden crash when John slammed his fist on the white ivories and lowered his forehead to the top ledge of the piano. Heavy breaths rushed out of his lungs as if he had just finished a race.

"John?"

With a sharp jerk, he brought his face up, glaring at her.

"What are you doing here?" The harsh voice did not sound like the man she had come to know.

She took a step back. One thing she knew for a fact—men were unpredictable, especially if they felt threatened.

"I'm sorry." She stepped back to make her exit. "I wanted you to know that Uncle Billy said we can use the cherry picker." She started to turn but paused. An overwhelming longing made her tell him what she had just experienced. "You just played the most beautiful, compelling piece of music I have ever heard."

"Thank you." The words came from a still jaw. He looked back at the piano, his fingers casually running over the ivory keys and tickling little notes out of the old upright.

She swallowed. *Just leave, girl.* Instead, she heard herself speaking again. "Can I ask a question?"

Without looking up, he gave a half grin. "Sure."

"Do you ever play in church? I've never heard you."

He tilted his head back and combed his fingers through his hair, pushing the strands off his forehead. He shook his head.

Lorrie Ann moved closer, pausing at the base of the three steps leading to the platform. "I don't understand. You play music like that, but you don't share with your congregation?"

He sighed. "Nope." He started playing with the keys again. "I was hired to preach, not make music."

"Um…I think they'd be okay with it. Have you ever played in front of people?"

He laughed, closing the lid to the piano. John rested his

elbows on the wood and intertwined his fingers. "A few thousand."

"Really?" This man always surprised her. "I don't know a great deal about the Christian-music industry, but I think you're very marketable." She crossed the stage and laid her hand on the top of the piano. She knew music, and his was incredible.

"It's not what I want."

She knew people in the business that would give anything for a sound like his. "I don't understand. If you don't want to market your music, the least you could do is share with your church. Isn't there some verse about it being a sin when you waste a talent God gave you?"

"So, you're going to come from L.A. and give me Bible lessons?" Anger edged his voice.

She took a step back and closed her eyes for a moment. "You're right. I'm way out of line. Sorry I bothered you." She turned sharply to leave, acid burning in her throat. She was so stupid.

"Lorrie Ann, wait, please." John's voice followed her.

Before she got to the last pew, the tips of John's fingers touched her lower arm. She stopped but kept her back to him.

This man made her so weak. She didn't know who she hated more—him or herself.

"You have every right to speak the truth." His grip became a bit firmer as he silently urged her back to him. "We all need the truth. I've been hiding my music for five years now. Today, I couldn't keep it buried."

She focused on the tiny pattern weaved into the blue carpet under his boots. "I'm sorry I interrupted," she whispered. "It's not any of my business."

"I've played to crowds of thousands. Tears running down their faces, hands raised high as they sang the words. All that attention can be a bit intoxicating." John dropped his hand and stepped back, but his gaze never left her.

"You don't owe me an explanation."

"The truth has been locked up with the music for too long." He reached into his jacket and popped a Jolly Rancher into his mouth. "I didn't see my girls unless Carol brought them to the youth building. Ironically, the music became a stumbling block in my relationship with God. It ruined my marriage." He took a deep breath. "*I* ruined my marriage. I hurt Carol, who had given me nothing but love and support."

"John…" She had no clue what to say.

Moving away from her, he sat on the nearest pew. "I was lost, but being wrapped in a Christian label, no one knew it…" He swallowed and bit down the raw emotion that boiled up in his brain. "Other than Carol." He looked up to the cross. "When I saw her at the accident site, covered in the yellow sheet, I knew her death was my fault. My sin."

"Oh, John." She stepped closer, wrapping her warm fingers around the coldness of his hand. "It was an accident. You weren't even in the car. You know it's not your fault, right?"

He squeezed her hand. "In my head, yeah. But I also know I had pretended to be a man of God, while living for myself in complete and utter selfishness." He turned her hand over, running the calloused pad of his thumb across her palm before letting go.

He twisted the finger on his left hand, playing with a wedding ring that he no longer wore. "Carol knew and had called me out."

He looked back up and gave her a lopsided grin. "Like you just did. She was good at speaking the truth."

The sorrow in his eyes pierced her soul. "I didn't have the right to tell any—"

He shook his head, stopping her from finishing. "I've never told this to anyone. I'd missed our monthly date night. Again. So Carol left the girls with the babysitter and tracked me down in the music building." He took a deep breath, and his jaw flexed. "There was no yelling or crying. She calmly informed me she'd prayed while waiting and decided to move back to Clear Water. When I got my priorities right, she'd be waiting for me. Then she left." He sat up and ran his fingers through his mussed hair. "I went brain-dead." He snorted and cut a look to her. "Know what my first thought was?"

Lorrie Ann shook her head and bit her teeth. She didn't want to hear any more. "I can't imagine." Her right hand reached out and took hold of his.

"I panicked at how others would react. The negative image it would create for me." He stood. "My wife was so hurt. She'd just left me, and all I cared about? How it would look to others." He moved to the piano.

Lorrie Ann followed him. Her cracked heart completely shattered.

"I knew right then I hadn't been living to God's glory but my own. I rushed out to follow her, to tell her I'd been wrong. To fix the mess I'd made. But I came up to the accident."

Her heart seized. "Oh, no, John. Don't. It's not your fault. Do you really believe God punished you by killing Carol?"

John stood before the stained-glass cross. His throat worked, trying to swallow. "No, but…" He walked back to the piano, running his hand along the top. "I blamed the music." He gave her a sad grin that pulled at her heart. "I guess it's my self-imposed punishment—no music and no love."

She moved to stand with him. "John, that's crazy. You managed to cut music from your life, but love? You're the most loving man I know. I've seen you with your girls, the people of this town, even the dragon ladies. The love you have for God is in everything you do." She smiled at him, wishing he could see the hope he had given her. "You seem to have an endless amount of love."

He grunted. "*Love* is a loaded word. I *do* love my girls. I love the Lord, love my life here in this small country town." He picked up a guitar and sat down on a stool. His fingers softly strummed the strings. "But a wife? I've destroyed one woman's life because of my selfishness. My heart can't risk it again. I can't risk someone loving me like that again."

Between his stark words and lonely chords, sadness covered her like a humid, sticky fog. This man deserved to be loved by someone who would share his burdens. That wasn't her. "What made you play today?"

"In the hall, a friend ambushed me, wanting advice about his wife." He paused. "No one knows Carol was leaving me. People talk about what a perfect couple we made." He focused on the strings for a moment. "I don't give marriage advice. It makes me feel a little hypocritical. I told him not to take love for granted."

"Not long ago you told me it is our imperfection that enables God to use us to help others." She sat on the piano bench, careful not to touch him but wanting to be close.

He shook his head, and a halfhearted grin pulled at the corners of his mouth. "No fair. I turned to music when I lost my parents. Playing was my conversation with God. I could write about emotions and fears. They would pour through the instruments."

"The music I heard earlier moved me. I felt God."

"Actually, an old friend recently pointed out the selfishness of not sharing with my girls and the church."

"He's right. Rachel has the most amazing voice. Do you sing?"

He gave a slight nod, and she suspected his voice was as spectacular as his playing.

She continued, "Have you seen Celeste? She's already learned some basic chords just from watching Kenny on the piano. You have to share your talent with them, John."

"Yes, ma'am." He focused on his hands for a moment and once again changed the tempo of the song.

She sat back and enjoyed the music, his music.

He whispered low, "Thank you. Carol had no problem setting me straight either. It can be difficult in Cold Water. Everybody knew her from the time she was born. I didn't want them to know how I'd failed her."

"You weren't a bad husband, just a man, a very young one." She felt a little jealous of Carol knowing this man's love. How pathetic was that?

He snorted. "Thanks for that vote of confidence. Why do I get the feeling that's not a compliment?"

"Hey!" She threw a wadded piece of paper at him. Her heart melted when he chuckled. She watched his fingers drift back to the strings. This man deserved to be loved with a whole heart. Not the tarnished, damaged one that beat in her chest.

"You play?" Mrs. Miller's voice suddenly boomed from the double doors, a fierce scowl puckering her face. The disapproving energy crushed the fragile mood.

"Yes, ma'am," John answered with a heavy sigh.

Her cane thumped the floor with each step. "Why haven't you led the worship music?" her voice snapped.

"I was hired to preach." He gave her a gentle smile.

Lorrie Ann loved how he treated everyone with respect and tenderness, even the dragons. She didn't have the tolerance, another reason she didn't belong with him.

"Pish!" The old Dragon Queen gave a final stomp of her cane. "Pastor Levi, this is not your highfalutin big-city church. You have more than one job."

"Yes, ma'am. Miss Ortega just suggested the same thing. Great minds must think alike." He dared to wink at her.

Mrs. Miller's frown went deeper into her wrinkles. "I heard a rumor. You need to know, I will remove my support if that Puente boy, with all the things on his face, is in the band." She glared at John. "This is what happens when you let people like her run things." Her nose went higher. "Their kind corrupts."

Lorrie Ann bit her lip and battled to keep the ire locked

down. Not trusting herself to speak, she focused on John. He moved closer to the old lady.

"Mrs. Miller, I appreciate your concern, but we do represent the body of Christ, and our doors are open to everyone." John patted her arm and led her back to the foyer.

Lorrie Ann collected herself and joined them. *Please, Lord, give me the right thing to say. I need words from You and not my anger.*

"Please let me reassure you." She used her best smile. "Derrick will not be playing with the band. I hope you attend. Please keep us in your prayers. I believe it will be a special night of worship."

"Humph...we'll see." She stood tall and glared at John for a while. "Young man, you need to stay focused and not become distracted by things that glitter."

"You're not giving me dating advice, now, are you?"

"Humph! Better men than you have been led down the wrong path because of a woman."

"And hearts have been touched because of a woman, Mrs. Miller."

She narrowed her eyes. "Maybe." She cut her glare back to Lorrie Ann.

Lorrie Ann watched as John escorted the Queen Dragon to her car. He did love unconditionally.

With a sigh, she wondered what it would feel like to have someone love her that way.

She shook her head, disgusted with herself. All her life, Aunt Maggie had loved her, but because of old hurts, she had pushed her away. Just like Uncle Billy and Yolanda. They hadn't made her an outsider; she had done that to herself.

John returned with a big smile on his face. She sighed. Man, did she love that smile.

"Did I hear you lie to that poor woman?" he whispered.

"Poor? Right. Anyway, I didn't lie." She dramatically laid

her palm over her heart. "I promise he won't be playing *with* the band." She winked. "We have other plans for Derrick."

John laughed. "You are exactly what this town needed."

She smiled back. "God knew, I needed this town."

"Yeah, He's good that way."

She sent a word of thanks to God. Life was good—better than she'd ever dreamed.

Chapter Fifteen

Lorrie's life turned into a nightmare. In the morning, Melissa called from L.A. and informed her that due to the recent incidents they would be looking for a new manager. Apparently, some so-called friends had forwarded a couple gossip blogs about her and Brent's little scandal.

Oh, well, so went life in the entertainment business. She had already received some messages from other groups interested in her but hadn't returned any of the calls or emails just yet. What surprised her most? She didn't really care enough about it to be upset.

All her energy was focused on the current disaster heading straight at her. The locals liked to call it the One Hundredth Annual Christmas Pageant.

She now referred to it as her pending nightmare.

With coffee in hand, she looked over her list. She heard a truck pull into the driveway but didn't bother looking up. Uncle Billy must have come in early for lunch.

It surprised her to see John's boots stopping in front of her. Putting her laptop and coffee on the little table next to the rocking chair, Lorrie Ann stood. "Is everything all right?"

John nodded, his face grim. "I need your help."

* * *

"Sure, what is it? The girls?"

"The girls are fine." His throat locked up. This had been a mistake. He couldn't do this.

He glanced away from her, not really seeing the trees and birds past the patio but instead…all the time he had spent in the studio, away from his wife and family.

He needed to do this. *God, give me the strength to turn it all over to You.* "I need help with something." He turned back to Lorrie Ann. She stood with a concerned expression on her face. Her dark hair was pulled back into a ponytail, and she had no makeup on. She really had no idea how beautiful she looked without all the extras.

Sighing, he forced himself to focus on the reason he'd come to her. "Do you have some free time now? If not I can come back later."

"Oh, no, it's fine. I can help you now."

He found he couldn't talk, so he settled for nodding and heading back to his truck. Her steps quickly followed behind him. Holding the passenger door open, he waited for her to settle in before closing the door and getting into the driver's side. The journey began.

After a few minutes of engine-rumbling silence, she turned to him. "You should know I'm not in the habit of jumping into a car without knowing where I'm going." Silence sat between them. "Any hint as to where you're taking me?"

"I have to get something, and I don't think I can do it alone." His knuckles turned white on the steering wheel.

She sat silently again, waiting as they continued the drive. He finally veered through the big gates of his father-in-law's ranch. Taking the winding road past the main house, John pulled up to one of the bunkhouses in the back.

More silence as they sat there. He ran his hands over the worn steering wheel, feeling the cracks. Fear and guilt choked him. *Okay, God, I know those feelings aren't from You.*

Lorrie Ann reached across the bench seat and touched his arm. "John, you're starting to make me nervous. Why are we here? What do you need me to do?"

She trusted him, and he knew that didn't come easy for her. He was suffused with more guilt as he thought about her mother. He couldn't even think of any type of relationship with her while that hung over them.

Taking the keys out of the ignition, John separated one of them and handed it to her. "I need you to unlock the door for me."

"Okay. Can you tell me why?"

He didn't look at her, shaking his head as he climbed out and walked toward the porch. Pausing at the bottom step, he rested his hand on the rough railing. It was past time to unlock the door. Once the decision was made he thought it would have been easier. Did it make him weak that he needed her here, to get him over the threshold?

Lorrie Ann walked past, pausing before going up the steps. She looked up at him. "Are you sure everything's all right?"

He nodded, not even bothering to try to speak. His heart pounded against his chest, and his hands started to shake a bit. It had been over four years since he'd taken the walk down these steps.

Lorrie Ann stood at the door, and after a few seconds of wrestling with the lock, she pushed it open. Turning back to him, she waited.

"Thank you." His voice croaked, raw with emotion. Easing through the door, he focused on Lorrie Ann's presence.

Musical equipment covered the wood floor, carefully boxed and stacked against the bare walls. He watched her walk through the dust particles that floated in the beams of sunlight.

Following her, he brushed calloused fingertips over the amps, drums and boxed-up soundboards. John tried to swallow, but his throat didn't seem to work.

"You have enough equipment to start a band." She pivoted around.

John couldn't speak. This was the right thing, and he was glad they were doing it together. With a sigh, he picked up one of the smaller boxes and handed it to Lorrie Ann.

Clearing his throat, he managed to get some words out. "Thanks for unlocking the door. I didn't think I could do it by myself. I'm taking all this stuff to the church."

She nodded and followed him. In silence they loaded one box after another. He stopped after the fourth trip. Seeing each box placed in the bed of his truck, he felt the tension begin to ease. Now for the big one. "I'll get the rest of these. Would you start pulling the instruments from the room over there?"

"Sure." She smiled at him before heading to the other door, not asking a single question.

While taking another load to the truck, he heard Lorrie Ann gasp.

John found himself smiling. He figured she'd appreciate what she found. As he crossed the room, his footsteps echoed off the walls.

At the open door, he saw her holding a black lid, the hard case containing one of his many guitars. Her eyes wide, she met his gaze. "Is this a 1958 Les Paul?"

He moved closer to her. "Yeah. I should take that one to the house."

She just nodded before heading to the quilt-covered grand piano. Lorrie Ann looked back at him. "Is this a Steinway?"

He grinned. "The one in the back is a newer Steinway." He joined her, lifting the custom-quilted cover off the baby grand. He played a few keys. "This is a 1970 Baldwin. It was a gift. It needs to be tuned. I'll probably get George to help me move them to the church. When the youth building's finished, I'll take them all over there."

He closed his eyes and listened to the sweet notes. A lightness settled across his shoulders. A weight he'd carried for so long he hadn't even noticed it, dissipated.

"Oh, John, this baby grand would be perfect in the corner of your new living room. I can see it right next to the office."

The vision flashed across his mind's eye: his girls sitting side by side, on a bench, playing music. "I always kept my music at the church. I didn't want the music to interfere with family time."

"So you spent all your time at the church." Lorrie paused. "Instead of isolating that part of you, maybe the music should become a part of your family."

He stepped away from the Baldwin without responding.

She followed him, her gaze roaming over his old life. "This collection of quality instruments tells me a great deal about the owner. Music is not just a hobby but in every fiber of your DNA. How could you cut it out of your life completely?"

Opening a violin case, he ran his fingers over the dark glossy wood. "Guilt. Easier to lock it away than deal with it." Raising his head, he looked into her sweet eyes. "Ephesians tells us, 'For by grace you have been saved through faith. And this is not your own doing; it is the gift of God, not a result of works.' When I cut music from my life I wasn't completely trusting God." He walked over to her. "The other day you said I wasn't sharing my gifts. I'd like to thank you for that, Lorrie Ann. I know you think God brought you here because you needed us, but God also brought you into my life. Because we need you just as much."

"Oh, John." Tears started beading up before she spun away from him. "I'll put these in your backseat. The kids are going to fall in love with them."

Yeah, and he seemed to be falling in love with her. But he kept that to himself, grabbing a couple violins and following her out.

Lorrie Ann looked across the field. Everywhere she turned, people were working. She glanced down at her list, so much still undone.

The donkey, Alfredo, only moved if you gave him a banana, but it disagreed with him, causing foul odors to fill the air around him, every time. Her fingers went to her forehead when she saw Celeste and her group rolling around like puppies again. The pressure pounded against her temple.

She looked down at her notes once more, hoping for answers. The lights guy still didn't understand stage cues, and Vickie argued over every costume idea. As of yet, Lorrie Ann had not seen one completed outfit.

She walked toward the band. Her solo drummer had pulled a disappearing act again.

Stopping at the edge of the stage, she waited for John to finish showing Kenny how to place his fingers on the strings of the new Gibson.

"Excuse me, guys. Have you seen Derrick?"

They both looked up at her, smiles on their faces. "No, ma'am, but I saw Carlos, so he should be around somewhere," Kenny answered.

She hated when they called her ma'am, but they couldn't seem to help themselves.

Humor flooded John's eyes as he smiled at her. "Your special project gone AWOL again?"

There seemed to be a new lightness in John since they had pulled his instruments out of storage. Sharing his music skills with the kids came so naturally to him.

Last Sunday in church, he had led a worship song. His voice had hit every note perfectly with so much emotion, everyone had stood in awe, forgetting to sing along.

With his influence, the quality of their sound would improve greatly by the night of the show.

That was the only thing going right. She looked down at her notes yet again. More question marks and concerns shadowed her script.

She reluctantly looked back to the stage. The worst part

of her life right now? She was totally falling in love with a man that could never be hers.

She checked her phone. She didn't have even half the to-do list done, and everyone was already packing up. Mothers arrived to pick up the younger ones, and she finally saw Derrick sitting in a truck waiting for Carlos.

She hurried over and smiled at him. "Hey, missed you. Have you been practicing?"

He nodded. "I had work to do for my uncle."

"That's fine. Your part is a solo. Just keep practicing. You'll make it for the full rehearsal, right?"

He shrugged.

"Derrick, if you need any help, all you have to do is ask. It's okay. People want to help."

He nodded but kept his face straight ahead.

"Well, okay." She patted the door. "Oh, look, here comes Carlos."

"Hello, Miss Lorrie Ann. Dare has been practicing every minute at home. Momma yells, but he just keeps practicing."

Derrick rolled his eyes and waited for Carlos to buckle up before starting the old work truck.

"Bye, Carlos. Bye, Derrick."

Carlos leaned out as far as the seat belt would allow and waved. "Bye, Miss Lorrie Ann. Bye, Celeste."

Lorrie Ann looked behind her and found Celeste standing there. "Hey, girl. You ready to go home? Your father has meetings tonight at the church."

"Yeah. Rachel is talking to Seth."

Lorrie Ann frantically scanned the area, tracking down Rachel and Seth. They sat at the piano, laughing. She grabbed Celeste's hand and rushed toward them. A groan escaped her throat when she saw John make his way to the pair.

He laughed at something Seth said, causing Rachel to glare at her father. Seth slid off the bench and shook John's hand. He moved away from them, walking backward. With a silly smile on his face, Seth missed the step and lost his balance. Rachel gasped and jumped up, reaching for her crutch.

Vickie stood by the storage door. "Seth, stop being an idiot and get to the car." She stomped off without another word.

John stood over Seth with his hand out. "Are you okay, Seth?"

"Yes, sir." He took the offered hand, his face redder than a fresh strawberry.

"Welcome to the man club. Beautiful girls turn us all into goofs." John patted him on the shoulder.

"Daddy!" Horror filled Rachel's face.

John laughed and rubbed the top of her head. "Sweetheart, it's time for y'all to head home. I have a building meeting tonight." He hugged Celeste and winked at Lorrie Ann. "I'll see you when I get home."

She raised her eyebrows. His mood seemed different tonight.

"See ya." She reached for Celeste's hand and headed to her car. Rachel pouted as she climbed into the front seat.

Lorrie Ann sighed as she headed home.

Home. Oh, man. When had John and his girls so completely slipped into her heart? When had the cabin become home?

She thought about the contacts in California, waiting for her reply. Time had run out. She couldn't afford to play house with John any longer.

John's boots hit the top step. If anyone asked him about his faith, he told them he'd turned his life completely over to God. For the past week his eyes and heart had been open to the punishment he'd inflicted on himself.

Lorrie was right, but he didn't know if he wanted to tell her. He smiled. She already seemed a bit bossy.

Working with the youth and music brought another worship experience back into his life. Threading his fingers through his hair, John interlocked them on the top of his head and gazed at the stars shimmering in the deep purple sky.

He should know by now God's timing was beyond his understanding but always virtuous. He needed to trust God's plans for him were good.

With a deep breath, John gave the stars one last look before turning to the cabin. He stopped and laid his palms flat against the rough cedar wood of the door. He pictured her waiting for him on the back porch and the two precious girls sleeping in his bed. He took a deep breath and prayed.

"God, give me courage to deal with what's in my heart. Lord, You know my soul and the fear I harbor. Release me from that burden so I can serve You more completely."

He put his hands on the doorknob and eased it open. Stepping into the hall, he checked on the girls. The night had turned cool, and he fixed two cups of hot chocolate before heading to the deck. He paused at the door and let his eyes drift over her. The soft light of the moon washed her in warmth as she leaned against the railing, face turned up to the stars.

"Hello."

She jumped.

"Sorry." He stepped through the door and handed her a cup with steam still swirling upward.

She grasped it with both hands and took a deep breath, pulling the warmth into her. "You read my mind." Sitting in the other rocking chair, she looked at him over the cup and smiled. "Thank you."

Smiling back, he took a sip before saying anything. "You were deep in thought when I got here. Girls give you any problems? Rachel still mad at me?"

She laughed, the kind that reminded him of softly playing Christmas bells. "I told her to get used to it. A father that loves his daughter should take every opportunity to torture the boys around her."

"Yeah, I thought about installing a rifle over the front door. Dub has an old twenty-two. I remember the first time I met him, he was cleaning it." Laughing, he leaned back in the rocker and took another sip. "Carol got so mad at him. Later I learned he never kept bullets in it."

Her laughter became louder before she covered her mouth and twisted to see if she had wakened the girls. "Sorry, that's just too funny. They'll appreciate your efforts one day, I promise."

He tried picturing his girls old enough to date and couldn't do it. He looked back at Lorrie Ann. She had one leg tucked under her as she rocked with the other one. She stared at the black-outlined hills while taking sips of the hot cocoa. Below the deck a deer snorted.

"So, if it wasn't the girls, what had you lost in thought?" The only sound she made in response was a deep sigh. Amazing how much a single sigh said while at the same time saying nothing at all. "Anyone giving you problems with the play?"

She shook her head. He knew sharing didn't come easy to her, so he waited.

Setting her cup on the deck, she pulled her knees to her chest. She wrapped her arms around her legs, making herself into a tight ball. He wanted to haul her up against him and promise her he'd fix it, but his own fears kept him out of arm's reach.

She finally turned to him, her cheek resting on her knee. "I got a call this morning from Melissa. The band has decided to hire a new manager."

"Oh, Lorrie Ann, I'm sorry."

She gave him a heartbreaking grin, the kind he now recognized Rachel used when she didn't want him to worry.

"Surprisingly, I think I'm okay with it. The whole messy drama with Brent had me concerned anyway."

Hope flared in John's chest. If she stayed here longer, he could take more time to figure out what they had. They could also settle the issue with her mother. She needed the truth, but Maggie had told him to hang on a little longer.

She faced out again, chin on her denim-clad knee. "With the rumors of the breakup, I'd already received a few inquiries." She smiled back at him. "In this business, you never know when you have to move on, so having options keeps you relevant. I'm thinking of taking an offer in Nashville."

With those words his hope died. *God, why can't something in life come easy?* Well, that was not true. His relationship with Carol had been easy, up until the point he had taken her for granted.

"As soon as the play is over I need to get back to my life. I thought it had to be in L.A., but I realized there are other options, like Nashville. Either way, I'm getting too comfortable here."

"What's wrong with here?"

"This isn't real life."

"It's real to me." He tried to keep the bitterness out of his tone.

"I'm not a part of this life. I'm just a guest."

John didn't know the details of her past, but talking with Sonia he could surmise it had been one atrocious event after another. He thought about that little girl, scared and alone, and he wanted to give her a home of her own, a place where love and safety lived in abundance. The question: Would she give up her music career to move here, permanently?

"You could be a part. Live here." He leaned forward.

She shook her head.

He had to convince her that the dream of a family was waiting to become a reality. He might not be telling her the truth about her mother, but he could tell her what was in his heart. "I'd like the opportunity to know you better."

She turned to him, eyes wide. Profound silence filled the space between them.

"No, you don't. I'm…" She gave a loathe-filled snort. "Stupid. I thought Brent would stop the late-night parties and take our relationship to the next level. We'd been drifting apart, not really connected. I thought if we got married… Well, classic female naïveté. I should have known better." She bit her lip and turned away.

John let the silence hang between them. His fist clenched, wanting to hold her.

"Man, was my timing off. He flew into a rage, one of the worst I've ever seen. He'd been mad at me before, but only when I nagged about his partying." She buried her face in her hands. A sob escaped. "In my head that sounded normal. I sound like a battered-women cliché."

"Lorrie Ann, your life is not a cliché." John couldn't hold back any longer. He moved his chair toward her until their knees touched. His fingers wrapped around her smaller hands.

Lorrie Ann studied the calloused hands in contrast with the tender touch John gave so naturally, making her want to curl up in his lap and hide from the world. He had to know the ugly truth about her. "His drug use had gotten worse. He was missing rehearsals and studio times, messing up onstage. I thought if we got married, started a family, he'd straighten out. He screamed at me that I wanted to ruin his life. I don't remember much of anything after he started hitting me and threw me into the kitchen counter. I pulled up tight into a ball and waited for him to stop. He kicked me a few times then left."

Somewhere during the retelling, John had moved next to her. His arms created a warm cocoon as he pulled her against him.

She rubbed the tears off her cheeks with the backs of her hands and pulled away, ashamed to look John in the face. From the corner of her sight, she saw him comb his fingers through his hair and take in a deep breath.

Reluctantly, she turned to him, shocked to see a tear run

down his cheek. She cupped his face with her hands. "Oh, John, don't cry for me. I put myself there. When he left, I lay on the floor, and you know what I did?"

His lips pulled tight in an angry line. With a slight movement of his head, he encouraged her to go on with her story.

She swallowed the lump in her throat, and her voice dropped low. "I prayed. In twelve, thirteen years, I hadn't talked to God once, but huddled on the ground, I asked for His help." She turned her face to the sky, unable to look at him as he heard the truth. "I realized I had become my mother. I had somehow become just like her. I checked for broken bones. I cleaned up and filled my car with clothes. I asked God to take me somewhere safe. There wasn't a single person in L.A. that I trusted." He took her hand and pulled her back into his warmth, giving her the courage to continue. Her face pressed against his neck, and she could feel his blood coursing through his veins.

"I was almost thirty years old, nowhere to go, hiding in a public restroom." A self-deprecating laugh escaped her lips. "You could say I'd hit rock bottom. And it wasn't anyone's fault but my own. Bible in hand, all I could think about was this purple-and-black afghan that Aunt Maggie made me for my thirteenth birthday. I wanted to pull it over my head and hide from the world." She rolled her eyes and snorted. "I thought I was too cool to take it to L.A. Stupid, huh?" She wiped her face with the back of her arm.

"No, I think God uses people and items to lead us. You'd need a reason to come home."

"Well, there you go. I'm sure you can find at least ten reasons the local pastor shouldn't date me." She stood up and moved to the railing. "So half the wild stories about me are lies, but it doesn't change the facts of my life the past twelve years." She took a deep breath, clenched her hands in the soft fabric of her skirt and slid a sideways glance at his beautiful face. She feared seeing loathing, or worse, pity. "I'm not the woman you need, John."

"Let God and me decide what I need in my life, Lorrie Ann. Especially what I want."

She leaned over the railing, listening to the water move over the rocks and around the roots of the century-old cypress. "The people of this church will never accept me, and if we date, everyone would think we're moving toward marriage."

"For me, marriage would be the goal."

"I can't be a preacher's wife." Her voice went a pitch higher. "People would stop coming to your church. They… would think you had lost your mind."

He snorted. Actually snorted at her.

"Maybe I have. Or at least my heart."

Her own heart twisted at his words. "Don't laugh at me. I'm serious."

"God knows you. You can't allow others to tell you who you are as a person."

"I know who I am, and more important, what I'm not. I've no clue how to be a mother. My own mother gave the world's worst example."

Guilt twisted his stomach. Maybe he should tell her now. He closed his eyes. It wasn't his secret to tell. He gazed at her, studying the outline of her profile in the moonlight. "My girls lost their mother, and I'm not looking for a replacement. She can't be replaced, but that doesn't mean they don't need mothering. Just as Maggie stepped in when your mother couldn't take care of you." He moved next to her, gently forcing her to look at him. "I want them to be around women of character and courage. You, Lorrie Ann Ortega, are a woman of character and courage. In spite of how your mom raised you—" he put a single bent finger under her chin "—or maybe because of her choices." He moved in close. His face hovered within inches of hers.

Lorrie Ann could feel his warm breath on her skin. Her gaze locked with his.

"My girls already adore you. You've brought silliness and tenderness to their lives. I tried so hard to be the perfect parent that I didn't see Rachel trying to be the perfect mom to Celeste."

She bit her lips and pressed her fist against her mouth. Swallowing hard, Lorrie Ann refused to let the cry escape. Despite her best efforts, she heard a pathetic sound slip past.

The worst part? She was sure John heard it, too. Her knuckles became wet with silent tears. She wanted to scream, but she knew that wouldn't ease the pain. In a last-ditch effort to stop a full-on sob, she squeezed her eyes shut. *God, please just make the pain stop.* "This is why I never, ever talked about the past. It can't be changed, so why relive the stupid heartache?"

John pulled her back into his arms. She couldn't stop the unleashing of emotion. The weak whimpering sounds became painful sobs, stuck in her throat, causing her to take large gulps of air.

"I hate this." *Breathe.* "I hate being weak. And I'm getting you all wet. Sorry."

"Hey, that's why I'm here."

She wiped at his shirt. "Being a pastor, you probably have to deal with people's emotions all the time."

"Is that how you see me? As your pastor?"

She laughed at the frustration in his voice. "You're so much more than just a pastor. I never dreamed I'd have a pastor as a friend. God knows what we need before we do, right? God knew no ordinary Christian could help me. My life needed a full-time professional."

His jaw flexed. "Lorrie Ann, I want to be more."

She shook her head. "I can't, sorry." Pulling herself away from his warmth, she forced herself to walk slowly through the cabin and out his door. This night he didn't follow her.

Chapter Sixteen

Lorrie Ann watched John lift a faux roof panel on one of the storefronts as Jake drilled the pieces together.

After she left his cabin three days ago, he stayed on her mind. The idea of being loved by a man like him seemed unreal. Then she imagined how his church would react and that was very real.

"Hello, anyone home?" Katy waved her hand.

"Sorry, I got distracted." She put her autosmile in place.

"Yeah, right." Katy laughed. "Pastor John seems more...I don't know, relaxed? Would you know anything about that?"

"I think music..." Before she finished, Katy swiped at Lorrie Ann's arm.

"I've seen the way he looks at you." She sighed. "He's such a good man, and being a small-town preacher has got to be tough." Katy looked over to the men assembling the stage. "It has to be a bit lonely. He can't really talk to anyone."

"He needs someone the community can trust, too." Lorrie Ann bit the corner of her lip. By leaving, she would be doing the right thing.

"They don't know you. Anyway—" Katy shrugged her shoulders "—God is the One we need to trust."

Lorrie Ann rubbed the palms of her hands into her eye

sockets. All this thinking formed a major headache. She needed to change the subject.

"What I need is a clean run-through. Why didn't someone stop me when I told Celeste she and a small herd of six-year-olds could open the play?" Ugh, another headache.

"I think we did." Katy laughed. "I'd be more worried about the foul odor your mood-setting donkey might bring to the manger." She wrinkled her nose.

"Oh, don't remind me." Lorrie Ann groaned then, taking a minute to look around at the unfinished youth building. "At least the building committee outdid themselves. If nothing else we'll have a great setting."

Three teenage girls giggled as they wrapped the metal poles in white icicle lights. In Lorrie Ann's mind, the jury was still out on tacky versus beautiful. It had been Katy's initiative, so she was willing to explore the idea. She glanced down at her clipboard. "Have you seen Vickie, or a hint of a costume?"

"No, but as much as she can be pigheaded about you, she would never do anything to hurt the play or the kids. You just gotta have some trust."

Lorrie Ann stopped herself from rolling her eyes. If she heard that word one more time, she might throw something.

Her gaze found John again. He had moved to stage left to erect the manger.

She smiled. She did trust him and her aunt Maggie. Maybe there was hope for her. She sighed and loosened her grip on her to-do list. She needed to trust God in all things.

"You're staring again." Katy bumped her and laughed. "You're worse than a high-school girl with her first crush." She took a sharp intake of breath before breaking into a giggle. "Don't look now, but guess who's headin' our way?"

Lorrie Ann felt her skin getting warm. She needed to get away from him. Fear of giving up her dream for him caused her throat to close up.

"Hey, ladies, I can't believe how well it's coming together." The devastating smile that wiped out all good intentions flashed her way. Did he even know what kind of weapon he carried?

Katy laughed. "Lorrie Ann's list of problems is still longer than her 'done' list."

Lorrie Ann glared at Katy and reevaluated the best-friend status she had given her.

"Just a little trust, Lorrie Ann." He winked at her.

How dare he wink when everything was falling apart, including her life as she knew it.

"We're so far ahead compared to years past, and this is the most ambitious show we've ever attempted. The setting is incredible, Lorrie Ann. You and Jake have outdone yourselves."

Katy looked around. "It's beautiful, isn't it?"

John bent his neck to watch the girls above them hanging the lights. "At night, all the white lights will be spectacular. Great idea, Lorrie Ann."

"Katy's idea, not mine."

Katy wrinkled her nose. "Are you sure it's not too home-fried?"

Lorrie Ann hugged her. "Nope, John's right. They're perfect."

Katy raised her eyebrows and mouthed John's name while batting her eyes.

Lorrie Ann cleared her throat, which to her horror brought his attention back to her.

"Are you all right, Lorrie Ann?" He stepped closer to her.

"Um…Pastor John, do you think we can have a full dress rehearsal next Saturday?"

He narrowed his eyes at her and tilted his head. "That's the plan, Miss Ortega."

Katy touched Lorrie Ann's arm. "I have to go. Rhody is taking me to a movie in Kerrville, *without* the boys. He says he has a surprise." She made a face. "Hope it's good."

John smiled. "I'm sure it is. Enjoy your evening." He glanced over to the stage, where Jake, Adrian and Rhody stood putting the last pieces together. "I'll make sure he gets home."

"Thanks, Pastor John." She waved.

"Lorrie Ann, about the other night. I—"

She held her hands up to stop his words, took a deep breath and forced her eyes to look at him.

"Right now I need to stay focused on the play. But your words have planted themselves in my brain. I just don't know what to do about them."

He stepped closer. His fresh, masculine scent filled her senses. She closed her eyes.

"Maybe you should put them in your heart instead of your brain."

Her eyes popped open, and she moved back. "Maybe you should tell Rhody it's time to go home. Katy's been talking about their date nonstop."

"Yes, ma'am."

He leaned in, not allowing her to escape. The smell of his apple candy excited her senses as his lips fluttered close to her ear. "This isn't over." Then he turned, leaving her.

She watched him walk away. When she left town, a part of her heart would be staying here forever.

Lorrie Ann looked at her notes but didn't see them. Maybe she could stay here and see what happened.

"Lorrie Ann!" Aunt Maggie's voice broke into her musings.

"Aunt Maggie, hey, did you get a chance to talk to Vickie?"

"Yes, yes, yes, but that's not why I'm here." A huge smile covered her aunt's face. "I have a big surprise for you."

Lorrie Ann sighed. She hoped the great revelation would be a new donkey.

"Close your eyes." Her aunt disappeared behind a line of SUVs. "Are your eyes closed?"

Lorrie Ann rested her face in the palms of her hands. "Yes."

"Surprise!"

Bringing her face up, Lorrie Ann blinked in confusion. "Mother?"

The slim woman standing in front of her should look to be in her mid-forties; instead, she looked older than Maggie, who was fifty-two.

Lorrie Ann had to be in shock, because she felt nothing. More than fifteen years had passed since she'd seen her mother, and now, out of nowhere, she appeared. No anger, no happiness, nothing.

Lorrie Ann gave a small laugh. Last week, she had decided to forgive her mother for all the bad decisions, for putting men and drugs ahead of her daughter. What did God do? Plant the woman right in front of her.

Sonia crossed her arms over her chest and rubbed her hands up and down her bone-thin biceps, as if to ward off the cold that no one else felt. Lorrie Ann could see purple and pink streaks of color on the underside of her dark ponytail.

She darted her gaze to Maggie then back to Lorrie Ann. "Hello. I'm sure you don't want to see me. I… Um…my, you're beautiful."

A million thoughts ran through Lorrie Ann's mind; questions ricocheted across her skull. "Where have you been?" She noticed her mom looked clear-eyed. It was like trying to start a conversation with a stranger.

"I live in San Antonio. I've been sober for two years now." She gave Lorrie Ann a lopsided smile.

In shock, Lorrie Ann stared at the two women. "You've been in San Antonio this whole time? Sober?"

She nodded. "When I made the decision to get sober, I called Maggie, and with Pastor Levi's help, they found a rehab center in the Hill Country. I spent six months there, then eight months in a sober house. Now I have my own apartment and a job." She bit her bottom lip.

"I don't understand. Why didn't you call me?" She turned to Maggie. "You knew? The whole time you knew!" Shock flashed into hurt, but Lorrie Ann preferred anger. She glared at the women who had raised her.

"Hey, ladies." John's voice interrupted the scene.

It gave Lorrie Ann time to collect the pieces of her thoughts and put them back together in some sort of order.

She watched as he swallowed Sonia in a bear hug. "How have you been?" He then moved to Maggie and kissed her on the cheek. "So, you finally convinced her to come up and see Lorrie Ann?"

Lorrie Ann looked at him. She had let her guard down and trusted him. She should have known better. He had known all along. This was what happened when you trusted people. They betrayed you.

He looked uncomfortable. *Good.*

Maggie broke the silence that had started to linger. "I thought we'd surprise Lorrie Ann."

John's eyebrows shot up as he jerked around to Lorrie Ann. He opened his mouth, sure to say something wise. Lorrie Ann didn't want to hear it.

"Can we go to the farm and talk? If that's okay." Sonia's voice was hesitant.

Lorrie Ann wanted to get away, to get a chance to clear her thoughts. "Sure."

They moved to the car, away from the only two people she had trusted the most. Sonia continued talking. "I just need to say I'm sorry. There's no way to make up for the mess I made of your childhood, but…"

Lorrie Ann stopped at her door and looked over the car to the woman who had abandoned her to Aunt Maggie's care.

"Listen, I've lived in L.A. for ten years. I've seen what drugs and alcohol do to a person. That you've been sober two years is great." Taking a deep breath, she forced a smile, for now one of her practiced smiles. They both slid into the BMW.

"You know God's timing is…well…so God." Lorrie Ann backed the car out and paused. "A few weeks ago, I probably would have screamed at you or just stomped away in anger." She shifted gears and made eye contact with her mother.

Tears hovered on the bottom of Sonia's lashes, and in a raspy voice she whispered, "I deserve it."

John and Maggie still stood in the same spot she had left them. They stopped talking and watched her drive past, but Lorrie Ann kept her eyes facing forward. Silence filled the car.

For three hours she sat on the back patio talking with her mother. As a teenager, she'd dreamed about this. She might even accept God had put her here at the right place and the right time. Why fifteen years later?

"Mother, I have one question." She swallowed, trying to get past the dryness. "Why did you leave me?"

Sonia stood. Wrapping her delicate arms around her middle, she looked out over the hills. "You were getting older, and I feared that I would be too…messed up to protect you. Your aunt and uncle had asked to take custody of you from the time you were a baby. I knew they would give you a safe place to live, a loving home, school."

"Why didn't you say goodbye?"

"Oh, sweetheart, I had tried to leave you with Maggie and Billy before, but you would cry and beg to go with me. I always gave in, so I knew I would have to sneak out and not come back. I'm so sorry. You've treated me better than I deserve."

Lorrie Ann shrugged. "You're my mom." She had her answer to the question that had hounded her for fifteen years, and it didn't change anything inside her.

"Lorrie Ann, I know the hurt I caused you will not go away overnight. Thank you for giving me another chance to know you."

They both turned at the sound of boots on the gravel path. John stepped into the light. He cleared his throat and fisted his hands in his front pockets. "Ladies."

Sonia gave him a quick hug and said good-night before slipping through the screen door.

Silence hung in the air. John moved to stand next to Lorrie Ann and reached for her hand. "Lorrie Ann..."

She snatched her arm away. "You knew. This whole time, you knew about my mother being sober and in San Antonio, but you didn't think I needed to know?"

"Lorrie Ann, it wasn't up to me. Your mom was scared of giving in to the addiction again and didn't want you to know until she felt it was safe."

She crossed her arms over her waist. "I trusted you, and Aunt Maggie...Yolanda...you all knew!"

"Lorrie Ann." He reached for her.

"Don't. Stop saying my name. I trusted you and you lied to me."

"It wasn't our—"

"I don't want to hear excuses." She sat down hard and stared at the landscape but didn't actually see the beauty around her. In L.A., people lied, but you expected it. You worked with the knowledge everyone had his or her own agenda. "I've decided to take the new job in Nashville. They need me there in two weeks."

"You're just looking for an excuse to push me away. Don't do this, Lorrie Ann."

"Why?" She turned to glare at him. She had gotten too close and had made the mistake of falling in love. "There is nothing for me here."

She moved away from him and opened the door. Turning back, she forced herself to meet him eye to eye and waited for him to say something, anything that would convince her to stay.

After what seemed like hours of silence, she turned her back to him.

Before she started crying or did something else just as stupid, like rush into his arms, she snapped her body around and marched to the kitchen door. She didn't stop until she collapsed on her bed and sobbed herself to sleep.

Chapter Seventeen

"Lorrie Ann!" Celeste ran full blast and threw all her weight onto Lorrie Ann's torso, nearly causing them both to go over on the ground. "I missed you at our Wednesday-night dinner."

"Me, too, rug rat. I just had too much to do here." *Plus, I can't bear to be in the same room as your father.* "Are you ready to head home? You did a great job leading your group down to light the lanterns tonight."

"Rachel's in back with Uncle Billy and Aunt Maggie. They're decorating the bucket that'll lift Rachel."

"Let's go get her. You have school tomorrow, and this has been a long day." Lorrie Ann took Celeste by the hand and headed to the back of the stage.

From there, it didn't take long to get home and go through the bedtime ritual. Several times, Lorrie Ann caught herself wanting to hug the girls and never let them go. If she thought about it being the last time, she'd start crying.

Rachel wore a small brace now and could move much easier, so the girls slept in the loft again.

Slipping to the edge of Celeste's bed, Lorrie Ann pulled the cover up to her little chin and stroked her hair. "Well, you get the end of the story tonight." She swallowed the lump that suddenly clogged her throat.

Rachel surprised her by swinging her leg out from under the covers and sitting up. "No, Lorrie Ann, please don't stop tonight."

"But tonight the princess is reunited with her father. She gets to go back to his kingdom," Lorrie Ann whispered, praying she could get through this without crying.

Celeste clapped her hands. "Yeah, the bad duke is banished." She threw her arms wide, causing the covers to slip off her.

"Celeste, you are such a baby. Don't you know what this means? She *is* the princess. She's going back to L.A." Rachel crossed her arms and glared. "She's leaving us."

A sharp intake of breath made Celeste's mouth open, and her eyes went even larger. "No. You…you have to stay."

Lorrie Ann closed her eyes against the pain she saw in the innocent eyes. Maybe it was her own guilt she tried to hide. "Sweetheart, we always knew I wasn't staying forever. I have a new job in Nashville."

"But we're here. You can't leave us."

"Grow up, Celeste. People leave all the time. Momma left." Rachel's harsh voice became muffled as she threw herself back and jerked the sheet over her face.

Celeste cried out, "But Momma died." Her tear-stained face turned back to Lorrie Ann. "God's not taking you away, is He?"

"Oh, Celeste, I'm just going to Nashville. We can still talk on the phone, and I can even write stories and email them to you. I'm not leaving *you.* I just have to get back to my real life."

Rachel snorted under her sheet before she flipped her back to them.

Lorrie Ann sighed and drew the precious six-year-old into her arms.

"I promise I'll email or call every day if that's what you want. And I'll be back to visit."

"What about the play? You have to be here to see me light the way."

A hiccup from the small chest created the most heart-twisting sound Lorrie Ann had ever heard. She kissed the top of the small head as she stroked the silky baby-fine hair. "I'll be here for the play, then I leave for Tennessee. I'm so sorry, rug rat."

"You need to get over it. People move on. It's just life. Stop crying and go to bed."

Celeste looked at her older sister. "But you said that her and Daddy liked each other." She placed her little hands on each side of Lorrie Ann's face. "Don't you like Daddy? If he did something wrong, I'll talk to him. You don't have to leave." Her bowed lips pushed out in the saddest pout Lorrie Ann had ever seen.

"I do like your daddy. It's not his fault." How did you tell a six-year-old the problem was you liked her daddy too much?

Maybe for the girls she could do it. She closed her eyes. *Dear God, please show me what to do.*

She laid her cheek against Celeste and pulled her closer, smelling the fresh shampoo John used with the girls.

No, she needed to stop this. Once she returned to the music world, her life would fall back into place.

Soft sniffles created a pattern in Celeste's breathing. Glancing down, she realized the child had fallen asleep.

She slid the small body under the covers and stood as she pulled the blankets around her.

She bent down to kiss her and froze, remembering the first night she had seen John tuck the girls in. That seemed like a lifetime ago. With a light touch of her lips to Celeste's forehead, she asked God to keep the girls tucked in His arms and whispered, "Sweet dreams."

Standing, she put her hand on her lower back and arched.

"Good night, Rachel." She waited for a reply, but only silence followed. "Rachel, I'm sor—"

"Don't worry about it. I understand you have more important things to do than hang out in this middle-of-nowhere town."

Lorrie Ann didn't think she could have felt worse than holding a crying rug rat. Rachel proved her wrong. She moved to the door, stopping at the frame when she thought she heard a sniffle. "Rachel?"

"Night." A clear and decisive dismissal.

Lorrie Ann went straight to the deck, leaving the door open. Tilting her head back, she absorbed the sounds and scents of the night air. The water running over the rocks below calmed her. When she left, she wouldn't wait another twelve years to come back home.

Having a place to call home made her smile. She couldn't remember all the places her mom had dragged her to. Even in California, she'd bounced from hotels to apartments. She'd helped Brent decorate his beach house. It had never felt like a real home, no matter how much she tried.

John's little temporary cabin felt more like a home than all the steel and glass ever did.

She lifted her arms over her head and stretched. Bringing them down, she curled up in the giant rocker and pulled her knees to her chest.

Hearing the door, she twisted around to greet John but didn't see him. He'd probably gone upstairs first. She settled back in and waited.

What was taking John so long? Anxiety crawled up her spine. Were the girls still upset? She slipped her shoes back on and walked to the base of the staircase.

The moonlight cut through the darkness. Pausing, she tilted her head to listen. She didn't hear John or the girls. Scanning the room, she whispered John's name and waited.

Lorrie Ann moved to his bedroom door and softly knocked. "John?"

Looking toward the entryway, she noticed the front door slightly open. She had heard the door. Stepping through it and onto the porch, she scanned the driveway. John's parking space remained empty. Her stomach got tight, and she rushed back inside.

Breathe, Lorrie Ann. You're getting worked up over nothing. Nervousness pulled her skin tighter as she climbed the spiral staircase.

When she saw Celeste sitting up in her bed and Rachel still bundled under her covers, a rush of relief left her legs weak.

Celeste clutched her floppy rabbit to her chest.

"Celeste, sweetheart, what's wrong?" she whispered so as not to bother Rachel. Celeste's wide eyes darted to her sister's bed.

Her stomach started coiling again. Under closer scrutiny, Lorrie Ann noticed the form under the blankets didn't look quite right. Heart pumping against her throat, Lorrie Ann pulled back the covers, finding nothing but pillows and stuffed animals.

Her eyes flew to Celeste. Horror stories of children stolen from their beds flooded her mind. She reached for her phone to call John but realized she had left it downstairs.

"Celeste." She grabbed the girl by her shoulders. "Do you know where Rachel is?"

"She made me promise not to say anything." Tears welled up in her eyes. "She made me promise on the Bible."

"Come on—we need to call your dad." She took Celeste by the hand and headed down the stairs. As she reached for her phone, the door opened.

Hope surged through every fiber in Lorrie Ann's DNA. Instead of the missing eleven-year-old girl, John walked into the kitchen.

"Hey, guys. What's going on? Why is Celeste—"

"I'm sorry.... I was on the deck."

"It's my fault, Daddy." Their words overlapped.

"Rachel left."

"Left? What do you mean 'left'? An eleven-year-old doesn't just leave her house at ten o'clock at night."

"I put them to bed and then went on the deck to wait for you. I told the girls about me going to Nashville. They were upset. Rachel seemed angry, but I didn't think she'd run away. Where would she go?"

His face had lost all color as he ran his hands through his hair. He turned and looked around the room as if lost.

Then he pulled out his cell and called Maggie, asking her to start calling people on the phone tree. They would be meeting here with floodlights.

"How did she get out without you knowing?" All his words came between clenched teeth. "When did you discover she was missing?"

"I had my phone to call you. She must have left about ten minutes ago. She can't be far."

He opened his phone again and called Dub, the whole time pacing. This conversation was shorter than the one with Maggie.

He braced his hands on the granite bar, closing his eyes. "Please, God, be with her. Keep her safe and lead us to her quickly." He rubbed his palm over the back of his neck. "The thought of her out there alone..." He turned and headed to the front entrance.

"She's not alone, Daddy. She's with Seth."

He froze and turned to Celeste. Then his glare darted to Lorrie Ann. "Anything else I should know?"

"This is the first I've heard of her being with Seth." Celeste buried her face in Lorrie Ann's neck while she strangled the poor bunny in a death grip.

"Apparently, Rachel made Celeste promise not to tell anyone."

He walked over and stopped in front of them. Taking Celeste from Lorrie Ann, he gently sat her on one of the barstools and leaned in until father and daughter were face-to-face. His voice stayed low and tender.

"Sweetheart, someone can't make you promise to lie to your father using the Bible."

She reached up and wrapped her soft fingers around his stubbled jaw. "Daddy, please don't cry." She bumped her forehead against his. "And don't be mad at Miss Lorrie Ann. It's my fault."

He covered her tiny hands in his large ones. "I just want to get Rachel home. What do you know, monkey?"

"Seth threw some twigs at our window right after Miss Lorrie Ann tucked us into bed. Rachel went to the window. I couldn't hear what they said, but she told me to stay quiet and made me promise on the Bible. She said she'd be back soon. She wanted to talk to Seth, but he couldn't come in our room."

"Thank you, sweetheart." He kissed her on the forehead then stepped back. "I'll call Vickie." He already had the phone to his ear. Lorrie Ann blinked as each ring lasted an eternity. *Please, please, God, let Rachel be there.*

"Hello, Vickie. I'm looking for Rachel. We think she might be with Seth."

Lorrie Ann could hear the woman's voice, but the words sounded muffled.

"Would you check to see if he knows where she is, then?" He dropped his chin and rubbed the bridge of his nose with his free hand.

His head suddenly shot up, and she could hear yelling in the background.

"Vickie, calm down. Do you know where he might have gone?"

All Lorrie Ann could make out was something about his father.

"Maggie's already started calling on the phone tree. People

are going to be meeting here to walk the area. I'll call Jake and have him and his group meet at your house. We'll start walking. They should be somewhere in between."

Lorrie Ann heard Vickie's voice pitch higher.

"Florida? Why would he try to—" His sentence got interrupted. "Vickie, I don't think Rachel would run away to Florida, but she would probably try to stop him. They've been gone from here less than—" he looked down at his watch "—twenty minutes. We'll find them.... Okay. Call your parents. I'll touch base in a little bit."

He headed for the front door. "Will you stay here with Celeste?"

She nodded, not knowing what to say.

"I think Dub's just pulled up." With that, he disappeared out the door.

She hugged Celeste one more time. The little girl looked so miserable. It ripped into her heart.

"Can you think of anywhere they might have gone, a favorite place?"

The petite face twisted in deep thought. "They like to hang out at the swimming hole behind the big house." Her teardrops hung to her thick lashes, making her eyes look bigger than normal. "But it's dark, so why would they go there? We aren't allowed to go to the river without an adult."

Lorrie Ann didn't bother pointing out they weren't allowed outside without an adult and that hadn't stopped Rachel. She hit John's number on her phone.

"Lorrie Ann?" She heard a mix of hope and irritation in his voice.

"Is anyone heading to the big house?"

"No. Why?"

"Celeste says they might be at the swimming hole."

He gave a frustrated growl. "We just got lines of people walking the area between the Lawsons' ranch and the pecan farm. That's the opposite direction."

"I can take the dirt road through the orchard and check it out. Can I take your truck?" She needed to do something. Sitting here frayed her nerves.

"Okay, call me when you get there." The distress in his voice made him sound harsh.

"I will." He had already disconnected.

"Come on, rug rat. We're going to the swimming hole."

Seat belts locked in place. She made her way down the rut-filled dirt road that ran along the back side of the pecan orchards. When they arrived at the gate that joined the two properties, Lorrie Ann was surprised to find it open.

Going as fast as she dared, she finally saw the two-story limestone home standing sturdy in the moonlight. She put the truck in Park by the old stone barbecue pit and picnic tables.

Grabbing the flashlight, she slid out of the truck. Celeste followed suit on the other side. Lorrie Ann paused. What to do with her charge? Leaving her alone in the truck sounded dangerous.

Before she could decide, Rachel's desperate voice came from the river below.

"Rachel!" She yelled as loud as she could to make sure the girl heard her. The blood in her veins slammed into her skull while leaving her legs empty and weak. "It's Lorrie Ann." She broke into a run. "I'm coming, sweetheart."

God, please be with me. Breathe, girl. You can't panic now. Just breathe. Pulling her phone out, she hit John's number.

John answered before the first ring finished. "Is she there?"

"Yes, she just called up from the riverbed. There's a problem, so I'm calling 911." She ended the call and started hitting the next numbers.

"Lorrie Ann? Please, help me! Seth's hurt!" Gasps for air punched periods in the middle of her sentences. She sounded as if she'd been crying for hours.

"I'm coming, Rachel." Hurling herself down the old rusty metal stairs, Lorrie Ann prayed.

She swept the area with the flashlight until she found Rachel on her knees with Seth draped over her lap. His lower body disappeared in the water, and they were both wet.

"What is your emergency?"

"This is Lorrie Ann Ortega. I've found Rachel Levi and Seth Miller. We're at the old Childress ranch house down beside the swimming hole. I just got here. They're both wet, and he appears unconscious."

"I don't think he's breathing," Rachel cried, her panic-filled eyes begging Lorrie Ann to fix him. "I told him not to jump." She slumped over him and sobbed.

Lorrie Ann fell to her knees on the other side of Seth. She ignored the river rocks biting into her shins.

She handed the phone to Rachel. "Tell them what happened. I think we need to get him flat, but move him as little as possible."

She started checking for his pulse and any signs of breathing. Fear gripped her. Nothing. She couldn't find a thing.

Oh, God, please, please let him live. Please, please, please.

She pushed back the hair that clung to his forehead and looked up at Rachel. She spotted Celeste standing behind her sister, the stuffed rabbit held tight against her chest.

"Celeste, I need you to go to the picnic tables and watch for your dad and the ambulance. Okay?"

"Okay." She turned and headed up the steps.

"We have to start CPR." Lorrie Ann's heart pounded in her ears, and her limbs went numb as she pinched his nose and blew into his mouth. Meanwhile, she prayed frantically that someone who knew what they were doing got here fast.

A couple more breaths then she pressed on his chest, remembering the "Staying Alive" song the way her instructor had taught her. Her prayers to God never stopped. She knew

His power and strength kept her focused because there was no way she could do this on her own.

"Daddy!" Rachel's high-pitched cry broke through Lorrie Ann's focus.

Seth started coughing. Hope surged through Lorrie Ann as John came into her line of vision. He grabbed Rachel, kissing her on the ear.

"How is he?"

"He just coughed up some water. That's good, right? Should I breathe into his mouth again?"

"Have you checked his breathing and pulse?"

"I forgot." She moved back to Seth's face and bent over him.

John pulled Rachel to her feet. "Go up to Celeste."

"No! Daddy, I have to stay with Seth…"

"Go! Your sister's up there alone."

As she turned, the EMTs were heading down the stairs. Brenda led the group, and two others followed with a backboard.

Lorrie Ann had never been more relieved in her entire life. She stepped back as she answered their questions.

John's arm wrapped around her, and she pressed her back into his chest, the warmth of his body making her realize how cold she felt. His other arm held Rachel against his side. All three watched silently as the medics worked on Seth. He coughed up more water before they eased him on the flat surface of the board. With practiced skill, they moved him up the stairs, not one time jostling or bumping him.

Brenda approached the small group huddled together. "Are you all right, Rachel?" Her professional tone sounded calm and reassuring.

Rachel nodded. "Is Seth going to be okay?"

"We're taking him into town to be airlifted to Children's Methodist in San Antonio. You and Lorrie Ann did a great job. You gave him the best chance he can have."

Brenda led the small group up the stairs. At the top, they found Vickie in pajama bottoms and a large T-shirt, her tall frame swallowed in Jake's large arms as she tried to reach her son. Brenda rushed to them and quietly talked to the distraught mother.

Vickie closed her eyes and nodded to whatever Brenda told her. Jake's powerful arms slipped away, and the EMT led the subdued woman to the back of the ambulance. With the closing of the doors, they were gone.

Lorrie Ann turned to find Celeste and realized her whole body shook. Both girls now clung to John, and for a moment, she felt like an outsider that desperately wanted to be part of his family.

A stupid tear slipped down her cheek. She had no right to his family after the way she'd messed up tonight. She had no business trying to be a mother.

Maybe she should book a flight out sooner. They didn't need her here. Jake's authoritative strides cut the distance between them.

"Lorrie Ann, you need to sit before you fall down." Jake's command left no room for argument, but that didn't mean Lorrie Ann couldn't find any. With what she hoped was a defiant glare, she looked him in the eye and…collapsed.

John quit breathing and rushed to her side, pulling her from Jake's arms. He eased her onto the picnic-table bench.

"What's wrong?" Rachel's worried stare didn't leave Lorrie Ann.

The moan Lorrie Ann released twisted his spirit. She leaned forward, resting her forehead in her hands. Her fingers threaded through her hair, screening her face from view. He moved his hand to her back, needing to keep some sort of contact.

With the other hand, he pulled Rachel closer. She looked

so lost. Celeste squeezed between and crawled into his lap, pressing her small body next to his heart.

For a moment, he closed his eyes and thanked God for them all being safe in his arms. He prayed for Seth and Vickie.

"Daddy, I didn't mean for anyone to get hurt. I'm sorry." More tears ran down Rachel's already red and swollen eyes. "Lorrie Ann?"

Lorrie Ann raised her head. "It's okay, sweetheart. I just feel so stupid. I've never fainted before."

Jake took one step closer and sat on his heels. "It's a crash from the adrenaline rush. It's common." The trooper moved his gaze from Lorrie Ann to John. "They're airlifting Seth to Methodist. I called Vickie's parents. She won't be able to ride in the helicopter. Are you going? She needs someone with her, and I'm pretty sure that useless ex-husband of hers can't make it." He sneered the last sentence.

John sighed. They needed to head to the hospital. Vickie had a long night ahead of her, and she needed all the physical and spiritual support they could give her.

"First, Lorrie Ann and Rachel need a change of clothes before we go to San Antonio." He realized he assumed Lorrie Ann would come with him. She might just want to go home and burrow in her bed deep under her quilt.

He felt Lorrie Ann straighten. "Yes, we need to get Rachel out of those wet clothes. I…um…apologize for my little bit of drama." She rubbed her palm across her forehead, and he noticed it still shook.

"Lorrie Ann, thank you." His throat tightened. "I shouldn't have gotten upset earlier. I was—"

"You were worried." Lorrie Ann finished his thought for him. "It's okay."

"Well, I'll be going. Good night, and please let me know if Vickie needs anything. She won't call me."

John watched as the state trooper backed out and drove down the graveled driveway of the old limestone house.

"I'd planned to put a fence around the stairs to the river when we moved in here. I should have done it already." What he would like to do was build a twelve-foot fence around his girls.

"Daddy, I'm going to the hospital with you, right?" Rachel asked.

"Wouldn't dream of leaving you behind." When he stood, Celeste clung so tightly he didn't need to hold her to him, but he did. With a slight smile, he kissed the top of her head and moved to the truck. He had driven Maggie's golf cart, but he could have one of Dub's boys take it back in the morning.

"Daddy, is Seth going to be okay?" Rachel's whisper could barely be heard over the night sounds.

"All we can do is pray and trust in God."

A flash of anger crossed her face as she sent a glare his way. "You can pray all you want, Daddy, but sometimes bad things still happen." Her young voice sounded old beyond its years.

He focused on buckling Celeste into the backseat of the truck and prayed for the right words to say.

As he slid in behind the steering wheel, he found his daughter in the rearview mirror. Her face turned away from him and pressed against the window.

"Prayer and faith doesn't mean a life without trouble and loss, sweetheart. But it does mean you're never alone, even if the people in your life can't be there." He took a deep sigh and glanced over at Lorrie Ann. She had her arm stretched over the seat with her hand resting on Celeste's leg. He faced the front, looking over the hood at the trees in his headlights. "Rachel, life has brought me to my knees many times, but God is my strength."

He made eye contact with her in the rearview mirror. In her short eleven years, his little girl had experienced too many harsh realities of life. He knew a pat on the head and a reassurance that everything would be all right would insult her. "The hardest and most fearful prayer I've ever spoken was to ask for God's will to be done. I've never regretted following God. I have questioned many things in my life but never God's love for us."

She sat alone in the backseat, huddled in a ball. "Daddy, I'm so afraid."

"Let's pray." He twisted, and with his right hand, he entwined his finger with hers. He took his left and invited Lorrie Ann to join the family circle.

Her hand still had a slight tremble. He noticed Rachel's also shook as she reached for Celeste. He closed his eyes. "Dear Father, we turn our fear over to You. For we know You are with us. We lift Seth up to You. Your love will strengthen us and help us. Thank You, God, for holding us in Your hands. Amen."

Once at the pecan farm, it didn't take long to get Celeste settled in and find a change of clothes for everyone before they headed to San Antonio. He bent down to give Celeste a kiss.

"Daddy, can I go?"

"No, you stay with Aunt Maggie, but I need you to pray."

"Like the disciples in the garden? I can do that. Miss Martha said they fell asleep. I won't, Daddy. I'll pray for Seth."

John smiled and pulled the blanket over her shoulder. "Pray as long as you can then sleep. You promise to sleep? I don't want to worry about you."

"Faith means not to worry, Daddy."

He shook his head at the wisdom of innocence.

Chapter Eighteen

John's hand controlled the steering wheel as he eased the truck off IH-10 and onto the Medical Drive exit.

Lorrie Ann sighed. "Maybe I shouldn't have come."

He hated the doubt in her voice.

"It'd be an understatement to say Vickie and I weren't friends. I might be the last person she wants around her right now."

"You gave her son a fighting chance to survive." He reached over and took her hand. "It's a big hospital. If it becomes a problem, there're plenty of other waiting rooms."

She weaved her fingers through his hand and held tight. "I guess you're a bit familiar with hospitals. I don't know what to say."

"From experience, I can tell you there's nothing you can say. It's just about being there, so no pressure to find the perfect words of wisdom." He tightened his grip for a second before putting his hand back to the job of driving.

With a deep breath, Lorrie Ann tilted her head back and combed her fingers through her hair.

"That was a loaded sigh if I ever heard one. Want to share what's going on in that brain of yours?"

"I'm thinking your family would be much better off without me. Since my arrival, your girls have been in a car accident, the drama in the pageant, and I let Rachel just two-step right out the front door."

"Wow, I didn't know you were all-powerful." He found the energy to give a half smile as she rolled her eyes at him.

He pulled into a parking space and shut off the engine. "Lorrie Ann, God puts people in our path when He knows we're going to need them." He turned to make sure he had her full attention. "Did it occur to you that you didn't bring the bad, but you're the gift God sent to help us through these events?" He pulled her hand into his. "I know you can't wait to get back to your old life, but you've been a godsend. Don't ever forget you've impacted the lives of my family and others."

He moved in a little closer, their noses inches apart. "You got that?"

Her eyes turned a strange shade of grayish-green surrounded by the moisture gathered in the black lashes. She nodded.

"Good." He reached over the seat and gently nudged his sleeping daughter. "Rachel, sweetheart, we're at the hospital."

Climbing out of the truck, both girls followed John across the parking lot. As they walked through the sliding doors, John grabbed Rachel's left hand. He watched his daughter reach out to Lorrie Ann with her free hand. Joined, the threesome entered the children's wing, prepared for the worst, praying for the best.

Entering the waiting room, Lorrie Ann saw Vickie with her parents on either side of her. She tried to duck behind John and Rachel, but the girl wouldn't let go of her hand. She licked her lips and swallowed the knot in her dry throat.

Vickie looked up and, with a gasp, rushed them. She headed straight to Lorrie Ann and wrapped her in a death grip.

"Thank you, oh, thank you." Vickie started sobbing. "They said you saved him. If not for you we would have lost him."

Huge gulps of air filled Lorrie Ann's ear.

Not knowing what to do, she brought her arms around Vickie's shoulders. She made eye contact with John and gave him a *help me* look.

He moved in and gently touched Vickie's arm. "How's he doing?"

She turned and sniffed, wiping her eyes with the back of her hand. "Oh, Rachel." She grabbed the girl's face, cradling it in her hands before pulling her into her arms.

"How...how is he?" Rachel asked.

"He's alive." Vickie held Rachel at arm's length and brushed her hair behind her ear. "Thanks to you and L.A., he made it here."

Vickie pulled Rachel back into her chest and looked at John. "They're running tests on his brain and spine."

"Is there anything we can do?" John's hand gripped Vickie's shoulder.

"No." She shook her head. "We're just waiting and praying."

A doctor walked in, and Vickie's mother led her to meet with him.

Lorrie Ann found a lone chair in the corner. She leaned back, causing the vinyl chair to squeak. With eyes closed, she tilted back her head. The strong smell of disinfectant faded as she focused on the images of people, events, words and decisions that swirled in her brain, creating a whirlpool of thoughts. Her mother, Aunt Maggie, John, the girls and Vickie, the list went around and around until she felt the pressure suck her under.

John knew the truth to a life well lived. She didn't fully trust God, not with her heart.

Bowing her head in prayer, she asked for guidance. "God, please show me what You have planned for me." She waited. Opening her eyes, she studied her hands. *How do I know what to do, God?*

More silence. With a deep sigh, she closed her eyes. So, what if she went to Nashville?

Quiet, she waited and listened to her heart's response. The sounds of the hospital faded as the beat of her heart rushed in her ears. The girls—she'd miss Rachel and Celeste. She bit her lip at the thought of leaving John's daughters. They had taken a permanent place in her heart. She nodded.

Okay, what else? Images filled the darkness behind her eyelids: the river, the trees, Aunt Maggie's smile, Yolanda. With a sigh, she waded deeper into her consciousness and found her mother's sober eyes. A woman she didn't even know yet. Then the youth and all their music and laughter entered her thoughts. That surprised her. She'd discovered an unexpected purpose working with the youth group. A purpose she'd just found.

John. She bit down on her top lip. He felt like home. A home she never allowed herself to even dream about in her most secret desires.

Lorrie Ann thought of the new job in Nashville. She searched for anything positive. Nothing.

Opening her eyes, she scanned the waiting room and recalled her life in L.A. She had been spiritually dead. God had brought her here so John could give her CPR.

"Lorrie Ann?"

She jumped, surprised by the nearness of John's voice. She opened her eyes to look up at him.

"Can I sit?" He motioned to the empty chair next to her.

She nodded. "How is he?" *Please, God, let it be good.*

John smiled. "It looks like he'll be fine. Vickie took Rachel to see him."

"Oh, thank You, God." She reached out and placed her fingers on John's arm. The warmth shot through her. She pulled her hand back into her lap and hoped to give the impression of being unaffected.

She stared across the waiting room, not wanting to risk the

rejection she might see in his eyes if she declared her change of plan. Would he even care if she stayed?

"I'm thinking of sticking around for a while."

John's eyes widened. "Really? Why have you decided to stay?"

She bit her lip, twisting her fingers together in her lap. "I'm thinking it might be nice to get to know my mom."

His stubbled chin rested on his fist. Cutting a side glance at her, he nodded. "She'd like that."

"And I'd love to keep working with the youth, after the pageant's over. I mean, if it's all right with you."

He gave her a lopsided grin. "I think it's a good idea. How about—"

Rachel burst through the doors and ran straight to John. Wrapping her arms around her father, she buried her face in his chest. "He talked to me, Daddy, and made a lame joke."

John pulled her closer and smiled at Lorrie Ann over his daughter's head. "That's good news, sweetheart. Let's talk to Vickie, and then we can head home."

Lorrie Ann smiled back and followed as they walked toward Vickie and her parents.

She felt lighter. With the decision to remain, a burden lifted. She was home to stay. *Now, God, what do I do about John?*

Chapter Nineteen

The day of the play had finally arrived. Unlike Lorrie Ann, John had no doubt the Christmas pageant would be successful. He had other reasons to be nervous. He pushed the sour-apple-flavored candy around in his mouth.

He looked at his girls, sitting in front of him. Rachel, wise beyond her years, reminded him so much of Carol—not just her looks, but her mannerisms, too. He smiled at Celeste. Less than a minute of sitting and she already wiggled in her chair.

"Girls, you know I like spending time with Lorrie Ann, right?"

They nodded. Rachel's face became tight. "Just as friends, right?"

"I love Lorrie Ann, Daddy." Celeste kicked her feet.

Rachel turned on her little sister. "Can you sit still for five minutes?"

He pulled Celeste into his lap and, with his other hand, settled Rachel against his side. She grumbled, but nestled in close and laid her head on his shoulder. For a moment he savored having them close.

"After the play—" he took a deep breath "—I'm going to ask her to stay with us."

Rachel picked her head up. "But, Daddy, she's already decided to stay in Clear Water."

"No, I'm going to ask her to marry me and live with us at the ranch house."

Celeste jumped off his lap and wrapped her arms around his neck. "Oh, Daddy, she'll be my mom, and we can have sleepovers!"

Rachel pulled back and yelled, "We already have a mom, Celeste!"

Celeste looked at her sister in confusion. "But she's not here."

"Rachel, it's okay to love more than one mother." He knew she would have a harder time than her sister. Tucking Rachel's hair behind one ear, he brought her face up to look him in the eye. "I love Lorrie Ann, and I want to share my life with her. You're part of that life."

The tears hanging on her lower lashes sliced at his heart. "But, Daddy, I love Momma and I don't want to forget her."

"Oh, sweetheart, the human heart is phenomenal when it comes to loving. It doesn't kick people out. It just gets bigger. Your mom will always be a part of us, living in our hearts." He squeezed Rachel with his arm and laid his cheek against the top of her head. "You know what your mom is doing right now?" He felt her shake her head against his chest with her nose pressed flat. "She's scooting over to make an empty space right next to her. I can see her patting the seat as she invites Lorrie Ann to join her. That's what your mother always did, at every opportunity. She pulled people in and loved them."

"You think Momma would like Lorrie Ann?"

"Yes, and just because I love Lorrie Ann doesn't take away any of the love I have for you or your mother. It's just more love."

"I think Lorrie Ann would be good for Celeste." Rachel

pulled away a little and sat straighter. "You'll have more help. It's nice to have a woman to talk to about things."

John laughed. "Yes, it is." He kissed her forehead and pulled both girls tight within the circle of his arms. He flexed his jaw and sent a prayer out. Now he had to convince Lorrie Ann.

Chapter Twenty

The unfinished youth building had become a biblical village. Red-and-green Christmas sweaters filled the seats. Lorrie Ann nodded and smiled as people greeted her. A gentle breeze mixed the fresh outdoor smell with the aroma of the cinnamon snicker-doodles set out for the audience.

She glanced at the entrance and saw John shaking hands with each person coming in to watch the pageant. He looked over the crowd, stopping and smiling when he made eye contact with her.

He sent a slow wink that melted her spine and demolished all the tight nerves. She felt her smile reach her ears. *Oh, God, please wrap Your love so tightly around every heart here tonight, so all they see is the hard work the kids have put into the play.*

Mrs. Miller moved next to John, and the look she sent Lorrie Ann's way did not include a smile. Acid burned her throat as monkeys flipped wild somersaults low in her belly, pulling every nerve taut.

The list of things that could go wrong flashed through her brain. *We shouldn't have used the donkey. What if he does something embarrassing? The cherry picker might get stuck again.* Uncle Billy sat at the controls, so he would handle any malfunctions.

She glanced at John and wished she could stare at him all night, but her list called. Looking at her cell phone, she realized the kindergarten group should be lined up and ready by now. Lorrie Ann moved to the large panel off to the left, hoping to find them prepared.

Only fifteen minutes to showtime. The checklist scrolled through her mind's eye: the horsemen were in place; Mary and Joseph had Alfredo, the donkey; the choir stood to the right, their robes detailed beautifully; the innkeepers mingled with the crowd, passing out programs and offering hot cider. Pride filled her as they worked hard to set the mood.

Off to her left, the shepherds watched over their small flock. Some of the audience members had walked over to see what was going on with the herd of sheep. The band filled the night air with soft background music. Her blood rushed with the excitement of all the parts coming together.

Then her eyes went wide. She hadn't seen Derrick. She scanned the area, and her mouth went dry.

John had put so much faith in her. She had to make this right.

Behind one of the faux buildings, Lorrie Ann found Katy. Celeste and her classmates stood quietly, waiting for their cue to start the events of the night. She couldn't stop the grin.

Now she needed to find her drummer boy. "Katy, have you seen Derrick? I can't find him."

Katy shook her head. "He brought Carlos, but I haven't seen him since."

John walked over to her. "Everything looks great, Lorrie Ann." He smiled down at the short angels.

She skimmed the area. "I don't know where Derrick is. He should be here with the kindergartners, but I haven't seen him."

Carlos stood in front of them, tugging on John's blazer.

"Pastor John, I think he's hiding in the shed." He pointed to the storage shed next to the fence. His big dark eyes looked up to Lorrie Ann. "Sorry, he made me promise not to tell you."

She gave him a relieved smile and ruffled his curly hair. "It's okay. Thank you for telling Pastor John."

She headed toward the shed, covering ground in double time. John kept pace with her. She glanced at him. "We only have about ten minutes before you need to be onstage with the opening prayer."

He dared to laugh and moved closer to her. "In a hundred years, I don't think it has ever started on time."

She narrowed her eyes at him. Did he not realize how serious she took her job? "Not on my watch. I've never had an event start late. We *will* start on time."

His grin caused her to take a deep breath to calm her nerves.

"Yes, ma'am." He flipped his hand from his forehead in a small salute.

She didn't have time to reply as they came face-to-face with Derrick, sitting on a gray wooden bench. Knees pulled to his chest, he had his head against the rough wood of the storage shed.

"Hey, Derrick."

He jumped.

"Pastor John, Miss Lorrie Ann. I…um…I was looking for my drumsticks." He jumped to his feet.

John raised an eyebrow. "Really? You sure it's not a case of stage fright?" John sat on the bench and picked up the drumsticks. "The first few times I got up in front of people, I almost got sick."

"You?" The youth's lanky body folded back down on the bench.

John nodded his head and handed the wooden sticks to Derrick.

Misery and doubt clouded Derrick's dark eyes as he looked up at Lorrie Ann. Her irritation fled, and her heart went out to the vulnerability she saw in this teenage rebel.

"What if I mess up?" He looked down at his hands. "Some of the old folks don't like me. They think I don't belong here."

"They're not the ones to decide if you belong here or not." She cupped his face and brought his eyes up to meet hers again. "You belong."

John placed a hand on Derrick's slumped shoulder. "You need to remember you're not performing for the people in the chairs, not even for Lorrie Ann or me. You're using your music tonight to praise and worship God." John gave the teen's shoulder one last squeeze before standing to leave. "He knows none of us are perfect, Derrick. Just give Him one hundred percent of you. If you decide not to do this, we understand. One night doesn't make who you are." He looked at Lorrie Ann and winked. "Well, it's time to get this thing started." He turned back and handed Derrick a green hard candy. "These have always helped me."

Lorrie Ann watched as he headed for the stage.

"He's right, you know." Derrick's voice carried softly across the night. "Tonight won't make or break you. It's not your fault if we make a mess of the pageant." He popped the Jolly Rancher in his mouth.

A supple laugh escaped her lips. "Now you're giving me advice?" She smiled at him. "Good advice at that." She sat on the bench where John had just been. "By the way, I like your haircut. You have beautiful eyes. You also took out the piercing. Why?"

He shrugged and picked up the drum, running his fingers along the stretched top. "Didn't want to give them any more reasons to be mad at you."

Her heart melted. "Oh, Derrick, thank you, but you didn't need to change for me. I've been taking care of myself for a long time."

"Yeah, maybe you should let someone else help you every now and then." He flashed his seldom-used smile. "Someone told me that not long ago."

She heard John's strong voice quiet the crowd, and the monkeys in her stomach started jumping around again. She gave Derrick one last look. "Are you good?"

He nodded and picked up his drumsticks.

With a thumbs-up, she went off to find Katy and Celeste.

As she drew closer, Celeste waved at her, the long white drape of her sleeve flying with enthusiasm. No stage fright for this one.

Lorrie Ann smiled at Katy as she hugged Celeste and mouthed, *They look ready.* Ten little six-year-olds smiled back at her, their battery-powered candles ready to light the way.

Katy nodded and signaled them to turn on their candles. John said his final words, and as he stepped offstage, the overhead light went dark, leaving the kindergartners' candles as the only light.

Celeste led her group down the aisle, singing "The First Noel." Each student stopped at their assigned lantern that hung along the rows of chairs and in front of the buildings of the village. One by one, the lamps came to life as the children's sweet voices filled the air. They slowly disappeared behind the storefronts that made up stage left. Their song faded out.

Surprised at the overwhelming sense of pride, Lorrie Ann bit her bottom lip.

"They did great!"

John's whisper caused her to jump. She placed her hand over her rapidly beating heart.

He leaned in again. "Sorry, didn't mean to scare you."

Apple candy filled her senses. She smiled at him, and her heart soared, loving that he chose to be next to her as their little production unfolded.

In the heavy silence, people started shifting in their chairs. Anticipation of the unknown filled the atmosphere.

From the front entrance, hooves hit the concrete floor. People turned to see Alfredo the donkey led by Seth, playing Joseph. Sarah Garcia, a fourteen-year-old middle schooler, had been transformed into Mary, tired and miserable.

"Hang on, Mary. I'll find us a place to rest." Seth opened with the first line.

They made their way through the audience, stopping at each facade. Each time they were turned away. Finally they made it to the last inn, next to the stage. Alfredo, the sweet little donkey, plodded along without a fuss or rude odors. Lorrie Ann couldn't contain her smile.

They made their way up to the stage. The lights dimmed as the band and choir started "Hark! The Herald Angels Sing."

A spotlight found Rachel with large golden wings above the crowd. The audience gasped in surprise as they watched the cherry picker rise above them, cloaked as a white cloud.

Lorrie glanced at John and nodded with a full grin. His eyes glowed with pride, and he draped his arm over Lorrie Ann's shoulder and gave her a quick hug while staring up at his daughter.

The music faded, and Rachel spoke to the shepherds in a strong voice that brought good news and joy. As the light faded, the band and choir started "O Holy Night."

Horses' hooves pounded the ground from the outdoor area. People turned, and some stood as light flooded the right side of the grounds. Three riders, all from the high-school roping team, brought their horses to a sudden stop.

Bobby Gresham pointed to the east, toward the stage. "Magi, look! There is the Eastern Star we have been waiting for."

Kevin, his brother, removed his cowboy hat. "Where is the newborn King of the Jews? We see his star, and we'll go worship him."

The youngest of the trio and a cousin of Lorrie Ann, Rafe Ortega, swung his hand over his head, spinning his horse around. "Let us ride!"

Some of the spectators chuckled at Rafe's enthusiasm. All clapped as the three wise men rode out and the spotlight shut down.

The shepherds came and worshipped. The Magi brought gifts while the choir and band went through their songs. Rachel stayed overhead, leading the voices in praise.

The music stopped and the actors froze. Once again, the audience started murmuring. Whispers grew louder. Anticipation stirred the cool air.

Lorrie Ann bit her lip and reached for John. Would Derrick come through, or was it too much for him?

She looked up at John. His fingers interlocked with hers and squeezed. Then she heard it, the light tapping. It built as the drum moved closer.

As one, the audience turned to the front doors. Derrick stood still, playing a steady beat on his drum. The rebel teen's eyes remained glued to the stage, on the baby.

One boot at a time, he moved down the aisle. With each step, the beat became stronger. His voice joined the cadence, giving his only gift, the gift of his music.

Not another sound could be heard; even the animals remained silent. Derrick stopped in front of Mary and the baby. When his song came to an end, he bowed his head. The baby reached out to him, touching his hair. Derrick looked up to see the tears on Mary's face.

"Thank you for your song." Her soft voice carried throughout the silent building.

Lorrie Ann wiped the wetness from her face and realized many of the audience members had tears in their own eyes, including Mrs. Miller, the Dragon Queen.

Rachel raised her arms. "In the highest heaven, glory to God! And on earth, peace among people of goodwill!"

All stage lights went out, and the actors exited backstage as the choir sang "Joy to the World."

Lorrie Ann's heart burst with pride and happiness. She watched John make his way to the stage, giving credit to the members of the band and choir. He called the kinder group up and introduced each as they waved to family members. The actors came onstage, and he called their names. Derrick hung back, but John motioned him forward, and as he nervously stood center stage, the audience surged to their feet with applause.

Lorrie Ann clasped her hands together and brought them to her mouth. Her throat tightened as she tried to swallow. Derrick shifted his weight from one foot to the other, gripping the drumsticks tightly. She smiled and waved at him. He sent back a crooked grin.

John had the committees stand and acknowledged everyone who'd worked on the pageant. Celeste and her friend Carlos brought flowers to John, giggling the whole time. The pastor smiled at Lorrie Ann and waved her over. She shook her head, her muscles suddenly going numb. Could she refuse? She felt over two hundred pairs of eyes turn to her.

"There is one last person we would like to thank before we leave for the night."

Celeste jumped up and down. John laughed as he placed his hands on her small shoulders.

Swallowing, Lorrie Ann made her way to the stage, one slow step at a time. She battled a strong desire to run the opposite direction as fast as possible. Her skin felt too tight for her muscles as blood ran a furious race throughout her body.

She made sure to stay focused on John in order to avoid the stares of the townspeople.

He took her hand. "Lorrie Ann, you have brought so many gifts to our town and its people. But mostly to me."

To her horror, he dropped to one knee. She became immobilized; the crowd froze.

"Lorrie Ann Ortega, I love you."

The townspeople gasped as one.

"You have brought more joy and happiness than I thought possible. You already have my heart. Will you do me the honor of sharing my life and becoming my wife?" He held a ring up to her.

Her eyes went wide when she realized it wasn't just any ring but her grandmother Ortega's ring. Her gaze shot up to find Aunt Maggie standing with Sonia, offstage behind John. They had known? The sisters, both her mothers, stood in identical stances with hands clasped over their chests and tears in their eyes.

She forced air back into her lungs and looked down at John, still holding his pose. She saw his throat work as he kept his gaze locked on her.

She smiled.

He raised his eyebrow.

"At one time, you asked me if I could trust God," she whispered, leaning down. "Yes, I do. I love you and—" she swallowed the tears back and said the words that came the hardest "—I trust you." Pulling him up, she gave him a huge smile and cried. "Yes, I'll marry you—" Her words cut off when John grabbed her and swung her around.

"You scared me." He laughed.

The girls ran to them, Celeste's flowers losing petals as she squeezed tight. "We can have sleepovers now."

Her aunt, mother and cousin joined them, surrounding her in family love.

The audience stood on their feet, clapping and whistling. Some chanted, "Kiss her!"

John cradled her face in his hands and gently touched her lips with his. She closed her eyes, feeling cherished.

Someone else broke the spell by yelling, "None of that until the wedding!" Everyone laughed.

John rested his forehead on hers. "Are you sure you want to be a preacher's wife?"

"I'm sure I want to be your wife." She smiled at the rightness of the words. "I'll leave everything else up to God, including the dragons."

* * * * *

Dear Reader,

Thank you for taking the time to visit my small town of Clear Water in the beautiful Texas Hill Country. I'm thrilled to share it with you. Even though the little town is fictional, the Frio River is very real. Much of the landscape and a few of the places fill my own memories from childhood.

To share Clear Water's hundredth Christmas pageant with you has been a pleasure. I adore the Christmas season and all the traditions that go along with it. Between spending time with friends and family, baking the classic holiday treats and singing my favorite Christmas songs, I can feel the very creation of joy that makes the holidays something to remember.

In *Lone Star Holiday,* John and Lorrie Ann both have to accept God's forgiveness and people's love even when they don't think they deserve it. I enjoyed my time with them while they discovered the power of complete trust along the path to a new love.

I would also like to thank all first responders for their dedication and hard work, especially Brenda Gonzalez for answering all my questions about water accidents and airlift.

Stop by for a visit at jolenenavarrowriter.com. I would love to hear from you. The teacher in me would appreciate your opinions and answers to the discussion questions. Everyone gets an A!

You can also track me down on Facebook or Twitter.

Jolene Navarro

Questions for Discussion

1. Which character do you identify with the most? Why?

2. After the death of his wife, why was it a challenge for John to fully receive God's forgiveness?

3. As a child, then a teenager, Yolanda resented Lorrie Ann for her success. Have you ever been in a situation where a source of joy for others was a source of resentment for you? Explain.

4. What role do you think trust plays in Lorrie Ann's relationship with John, her family and God?

5. How does Maggie show her love for Lorrie Ann and Yolanda? Do you think both daughters were treated the same by Maggie? Why or why not?

6. Lorrie Ann saw herself as more of an outsider looking in; therefore it was hard for her to accept the love Maggie and Billy, then John, offered her. Do you see yourself as an outsider looking in or an insider looking out? Explain.

7. What was the turning point for Lorrie Ann's spiritual life?

8. On the outside Pastor John appears to have it all together, but on the inside he is struggling. What brings about the point of his self-awareness of his own lack of trust?

9. John tries to control everything because of his fear. How does this show in his life? How does it affect his relationship with his daughters?

10. Vickie takes her anger, hurt and bitterness over her life out on Lorrie Ann. On the night Brent came into the church, Vickie also attacked Lorrie Ann. How would you have reacted to her? Did John do the right thing for everyone involved? Explain.

11. Lorrie Ann's nonreligious lifestyle leads to spiritual bankruptcy. Do you think she needed to return home in order to reconnect? Can a religious lifestyle like Yolanda's or John's also lead to spiritual emptiness? Explain.

12. John tells Lorrie Ann God can use her mistakes and poor choices to help others. He doesn't use his own advice when it comes to counseling married couples. Why is it easier for us to tell others the truth but not show our own faults to others? Do you find yourself hiding some of yourself from others?

13. List one scene that stood out to you from John and Lorrie Ann's story and explain why.

14. *Come to me, all you who are weary and burdened, and I will give you rest.* Lorrie received this verse from Maggie when she was at an all-time low in her spiritual life in L.A. Have you ever received a note, verse or prayer at a timely moment, right when you needed it? How did it affect your relationship with God? Please share your story.

REQUEST YOUR FREE BOOKS!

2 FREE INSPIRATIONAL NOVELS
PLUS 2
FREE
MYSTERY GIFTS

Love Inspired®

Name _____ (PLEASE PRINT) _____

Address _____ Apt. #

City _____ State/Prov. _____ Zip/Postal Code

Signature (if under 18, a parent or guardian must sign)

Mail to the Harlequin® Reader Service:
IN U.S.A.: P.O. Box 1867, Buffalo, NY 14240-1867
IN CANADA: P.O. Box 609, Fort Erie, Ontario L2A 5X3

**Are you a subscriber to Love Inspired books
and want to receive the larger-print edition?
Call 1-800-873-8635 or visit www.ReaderService.com.**

LI13R

SPECIAL EXCERPT FROM

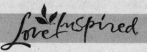

A shy bookstore employee runs into her youthful crush.

Read on for a sneak preview of
TAIL OF TWO HEARTS
by Charlotte Carter, the next book in
THE HEART OF MAIN STREET *series,*
available November 2013.

Vivian Duncan stepped out of Happy Endings Bookstore onto the sidewalk in the small Kansas town of Bygones. Watching leaves and bits of paper racing down the street, blown by a brisk breeze, she inhaled the crisp November air.

She hoped the owner of Fluff & Stuff, Chase Rollins, would help her put together a special event at the bookstore to promote books about dogs.

As she opened the door, the big green-cheeked parrot near the cash register squawked his greeting, "What's up? What's up?" He proudly bobbed his head and did a little dance on his perch.

"Hello, Pepper." Vivian smiled at Chase's recently acquired bird that was looking for a new home.

"Good birdie! Good birdie!" he vocalized.

"I'm sure you are." She looked around for Chase.

His warm brown eyes lit up when he spotted Vivian, and he produced a delighted smile. "Hey, Viv."

Smiling, he stepped toward Vivian. When she'd first met him, she'd thought he was an attractive man. She still did. At six foot two with a muscular body, he towered over her

LIEXP1013

five-foot-four frame, even when she was wearing heels. His short, dark hair had a natural wave that sculpted his head. His nose was straight, his lips nicely full.

"What can I do for you?" he asked.

"I, uh…" Snapping back from her train of thought, she started over. "Allison at Happy Endings and I have realized books about dogs are particularly popular. We'd like to put on some sort of a special event and thought you could give us some guidance about where to get a dog or two for show-and-tell. I know the puppies you have are from the local shelter."

Chase ignored the bird. "The shelter is getting over-crowded, so I've started a monthly Adopt a Pet Day here at the shop. In fact I'm having one this Saturday." He handed her a flyer from the stack on the counter. "And I'd love to help you with your event."

"I'm glad." She was relieved, too, that Chase could help out.

"When you visit the shelter you'll have to be careful not to fall in love." His eyes twinkled, and his lively grin was pure temptation.

Vivian blinked. Her cheeks flushed. Had he said *fall in love?*

Pick up TAIL OF TWO HEARTS
wherever Love Inspired® books are sold.

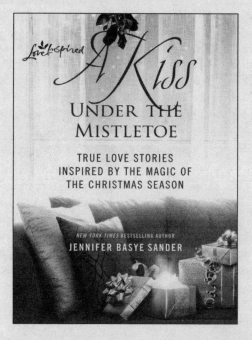

Christmas has a way of reminding us of what really matters—and what could be more important than our loved ones? From husbands and wives to boyfriends and girlfriends to long-lost loves, the real-life romances in this book are surrounded by the joy and blessings of the Christmas season.

Featuring stories by favorite Love Inspired authors, this collection will warm your heart and soothe your soul through the long winter. *A Kiss Under the Mistletoe* beautifully celebrates the way love and faith can transform a cold day in December into the most magical day of the year.

On sale October 29!

Love Inspired

During the Christmas season, Rebecca Yoder agrees to help
new preacher Caleb Wittner with his mischievous daughter.
Amelia's turned the community of Seven Poplars upside
down. Only Rebecca can see the pain hidden beneath the
little girl's antics—and her father's brusque manner. After
losing his wife in a fire, Caleb's physical scars may be healing,
but his emotions have not. Yet Rebecca's sweet manner soon
has him smiling and laughing with his daughter—and his
pretty housekeeper. Soon Caleb must decide whether to
invite Rebecca into his life—or lose her forever.

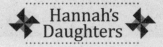

Hannah's Daughters

Rebecca's Christmas Gift

by

Emma Miller

*Available November 2013
wherever Love Inspired books are sold.*